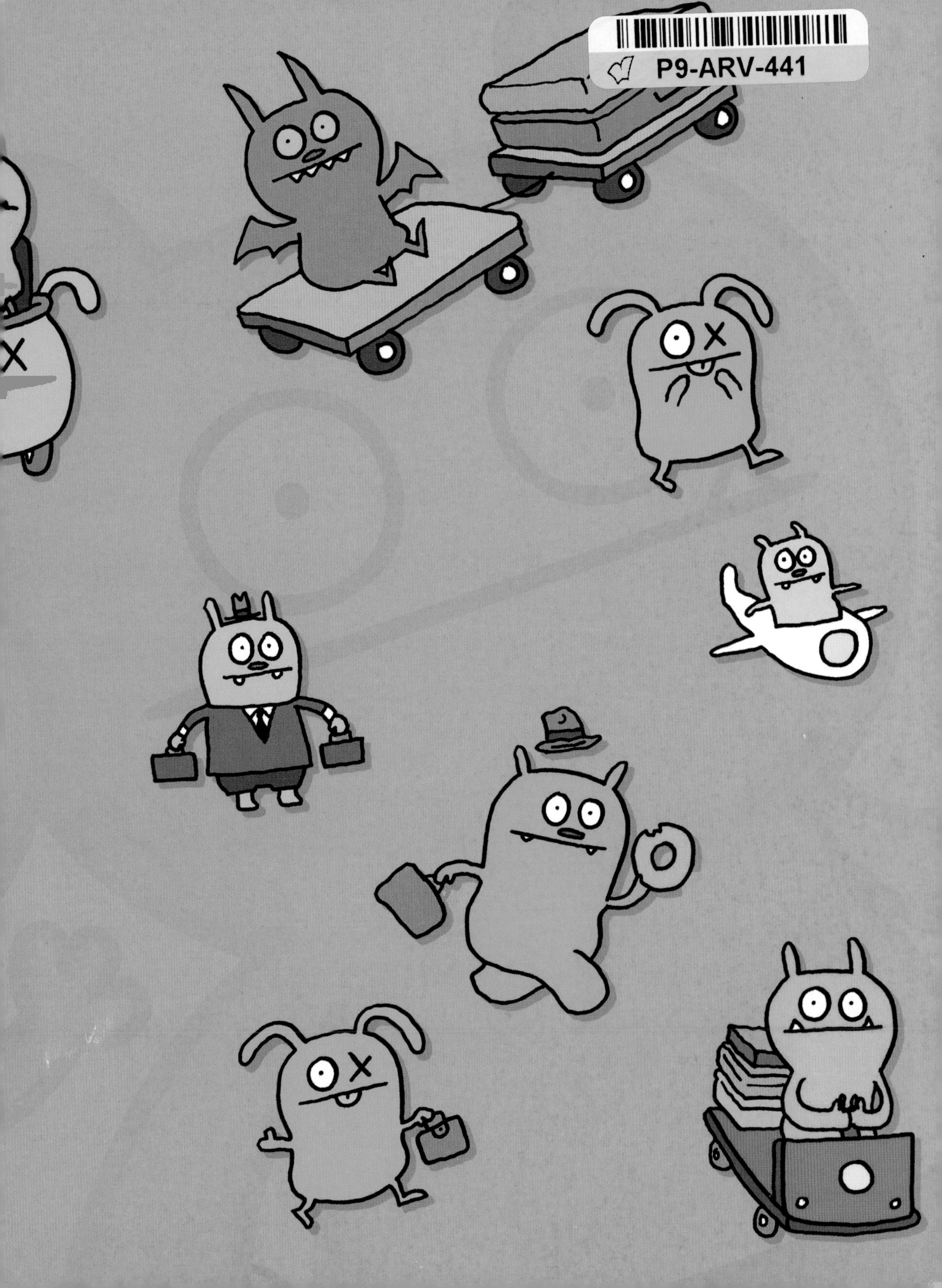

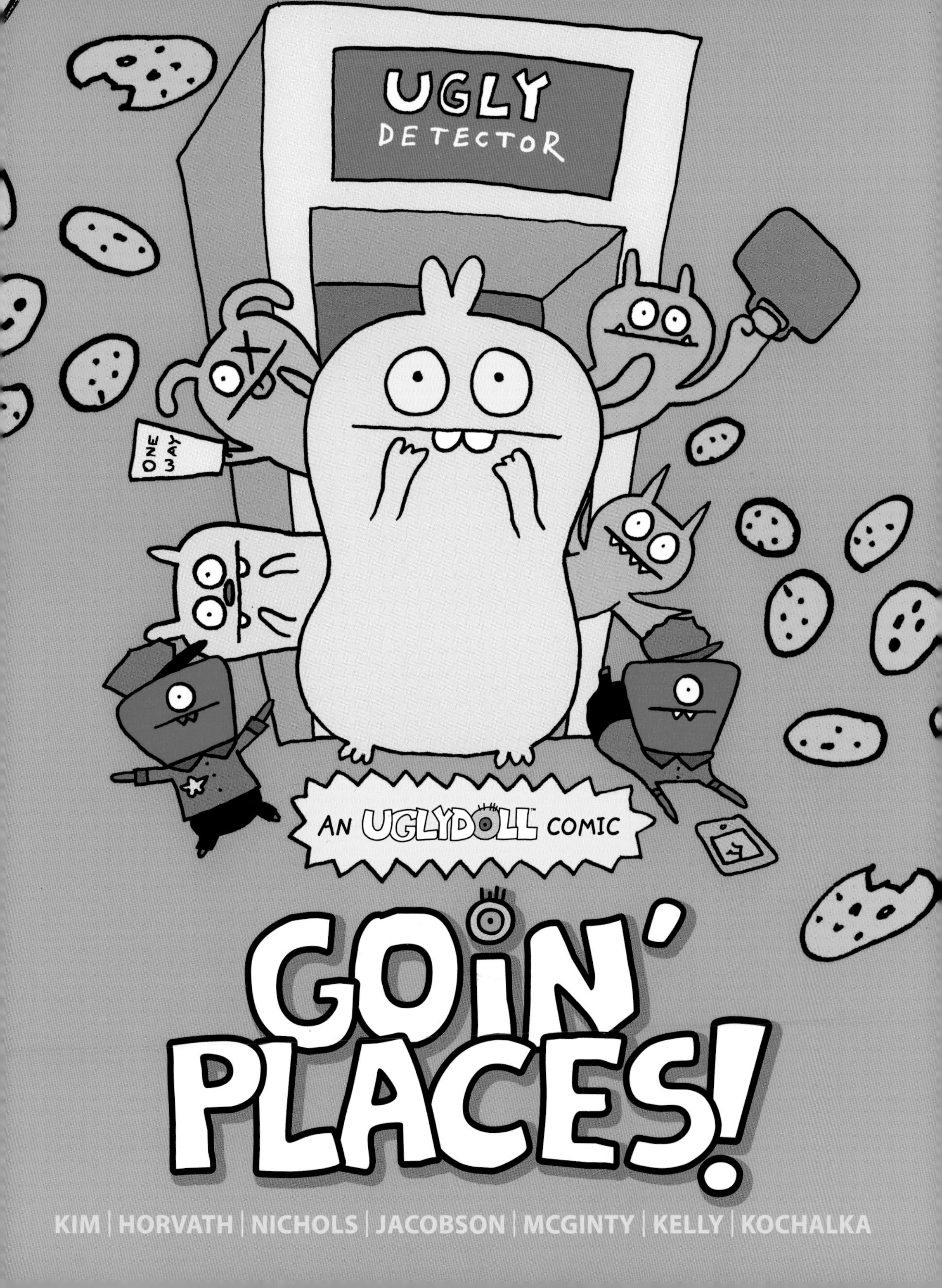
UGLY
DETECTOR
ONE WAY
AN UGLYDOLL COMIC

GOIN' PLACES!

KIM | HORVATH | NICHOLS | JACOBSON | MCGINTY | KELLY | KOCHALKA

An Uglydoll Comic:
GOIN' PLACES!

Cover Art: Sun-Min Kim and David Horvath
Cover Design: Fawn Lau
Editor: Traci N. Todd

Printed in China

Published by VIZ Media, LLC
P.O. Box 77010
San Francisco, CA 94107

10 9 8 7 6 5 4 3 2 1
First printing, July 2013

PARENTAL ADVISORY
UGLYDOLL: GOIN' PLACES!
is rated A and is suitable
for readers of all ages.
ratings.viz.com

WWW.VIZKIDS.COM

www.viz.com

Endpapers by Sun-Min Kim and David Horvath | **"Picture This!"** story by Travis Nichols, art by Phillip Jacobson, colors by Space Goat Productions, LLC. | **"Climb, Wage, Climb!"** story by Travis Nichols, art by Phillip Jacobson, colors by Space Goat Productions, LLC. | **"Get Lost!"** story and art by Sun-Min Kim and David Horvath | **"Ugly Old West"** story by Travis Nichols, art by Ian McGinty, colors by Space Goat Productions, LLC. | **"Once in a Blueberry Moon"** story by Travis Nichols, art by Phillip Jacobson, colors by Space Goat Productions, LLC. | **"Babo & His Bird and the Golden Cookie"** story and art by James Kochalka | **"We're So Bats Right Now"** story by Travis Nichols, art by Phillip Jacobson, colors by Space Goat Productions, LLC. | **"Ice-Bat's Cave"** art by Ian McGinty, colors by Space Goat Productions, LLC. | **"Ahoy, Me Uglys!"** story and art by Travis Nichols | **"Let's Go"** story and art by Mike LE Kelly | **"To the Top!"** story by Travis Nichols, art by Ian McGinty, colors by Space Goat Productions, LLC. | **Babo postcards** by Travis Nichols

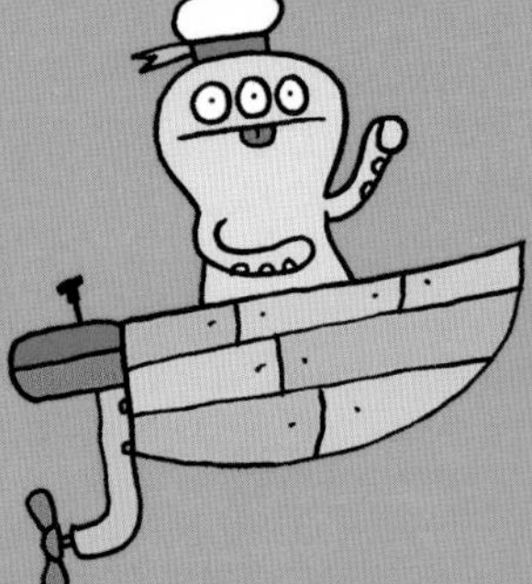

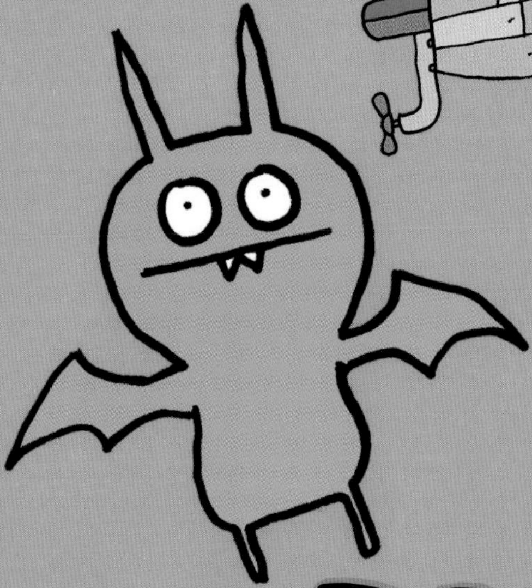

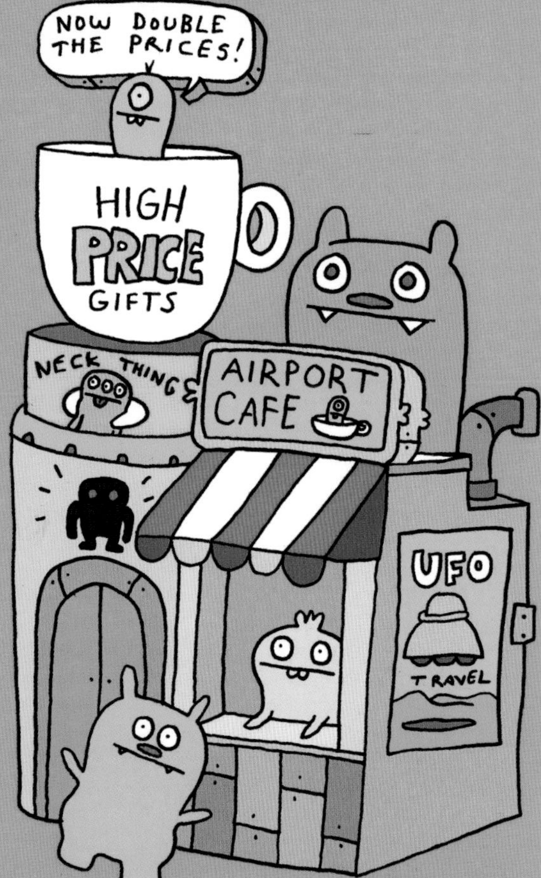
NOW DOUBLE THE PRICES!
HIGH PRICE GIFTS
NECK THINGS
AIRPORT CAFE
UFO
TRAVEL

TABLE OF CONTENTS

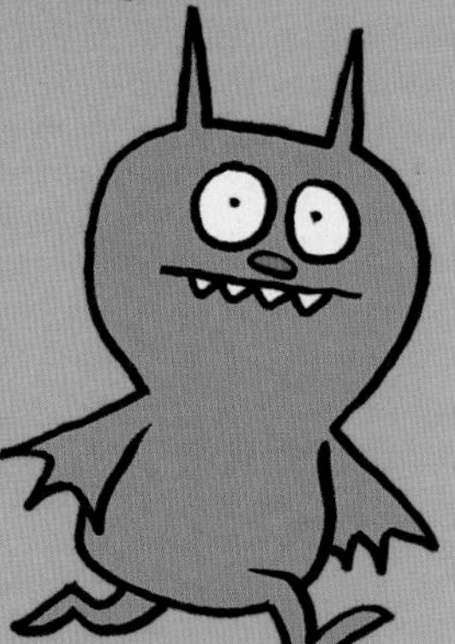

BABO

WHO

WEDGEHEAD

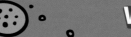

NINJA
BATTY
SHOGUN

ICE-BAT

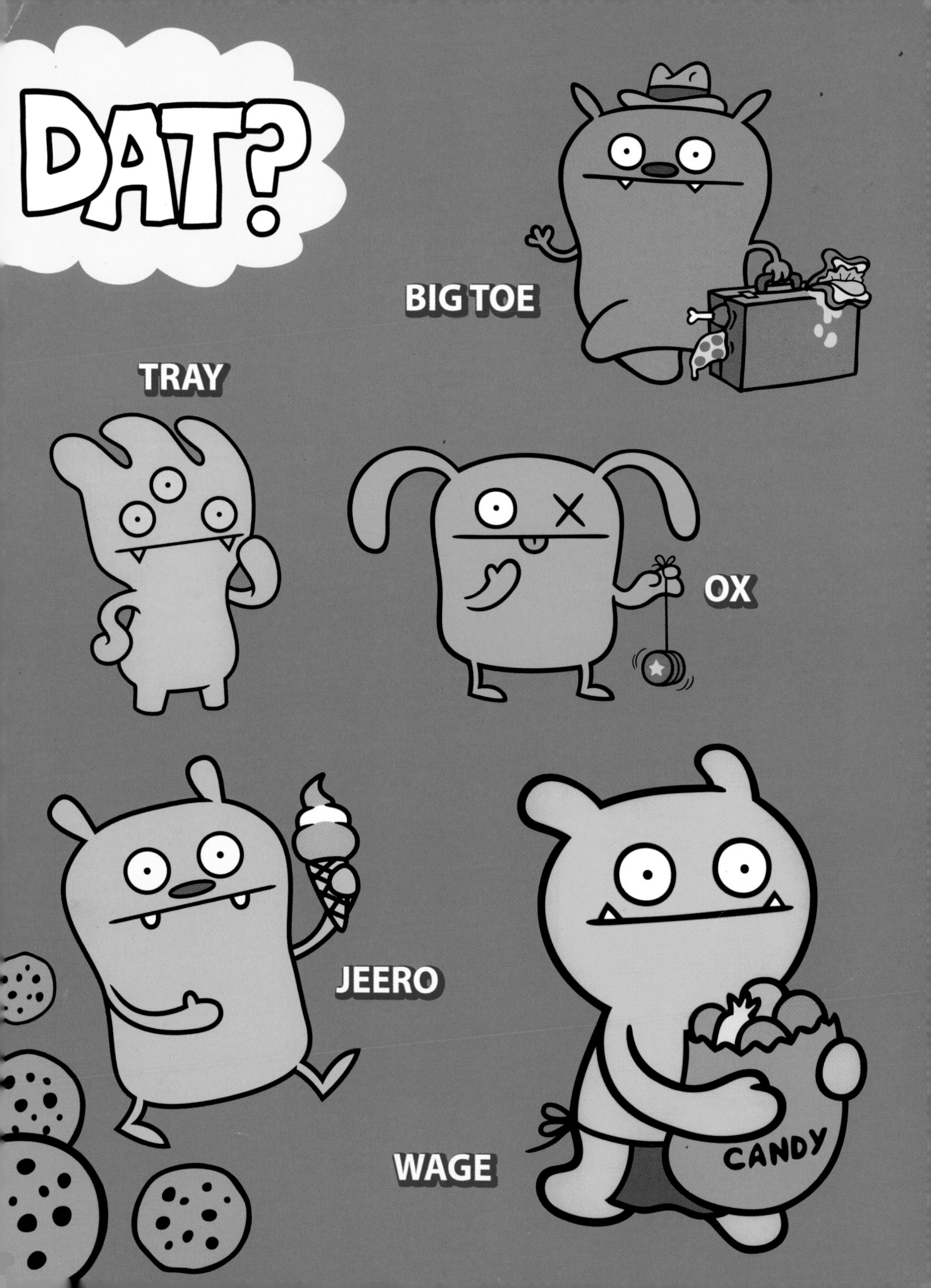
DAT?
BIG TOE
TRAY
OX
JEERO
CANDY
WAGE

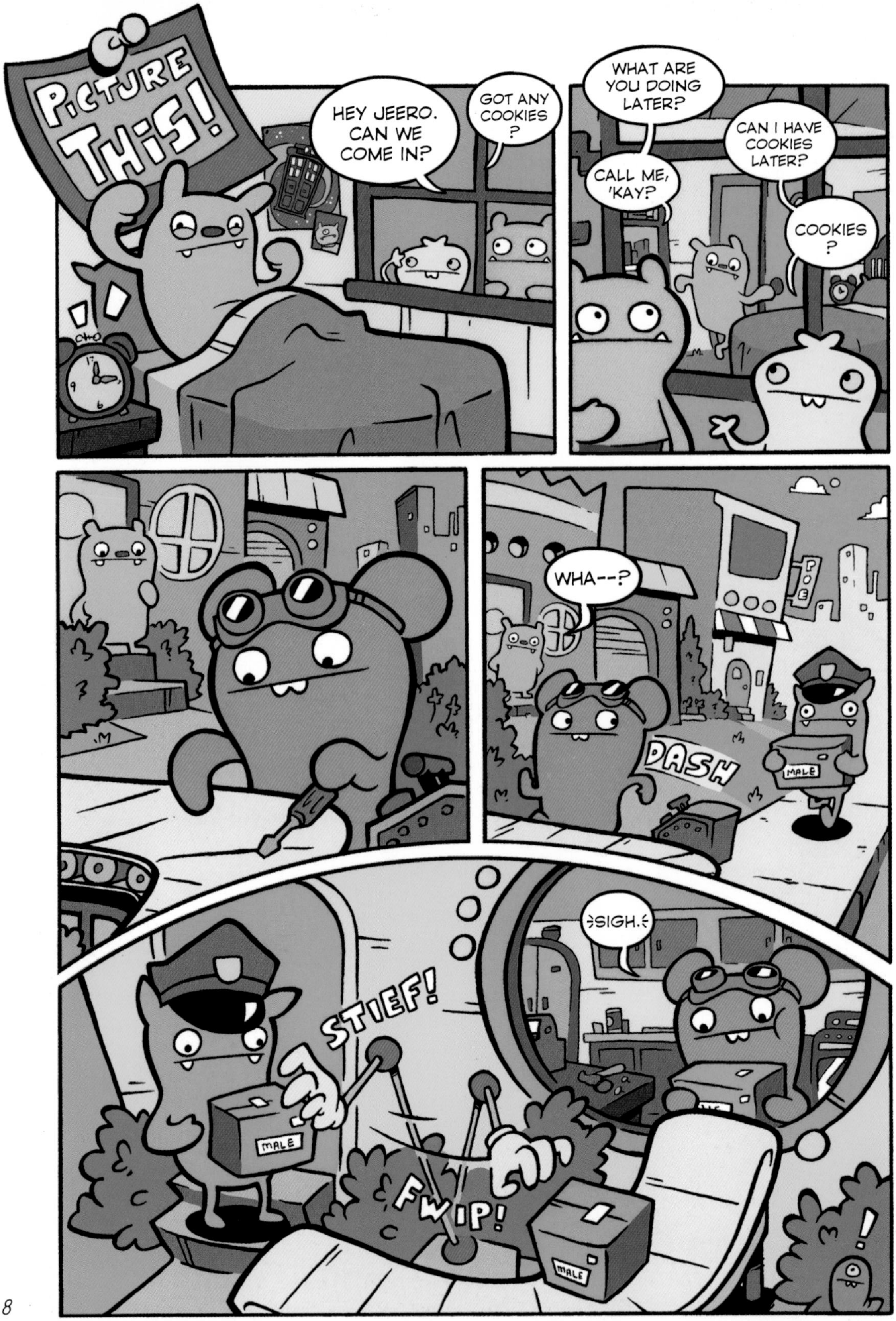

PICTURE THIS!
HEY JEERO. CAN WE COME IN?
GOT ANY COOKIES ?
WHAT ARE YOU DOING LATER?
CALL ME, 'KAY?
CAN I HAVE COOKIES LATER?
COOKIES ?
WHA--?
DASH
MALE
STIEF!
SIGH.
MALE
FWIP!
MALE

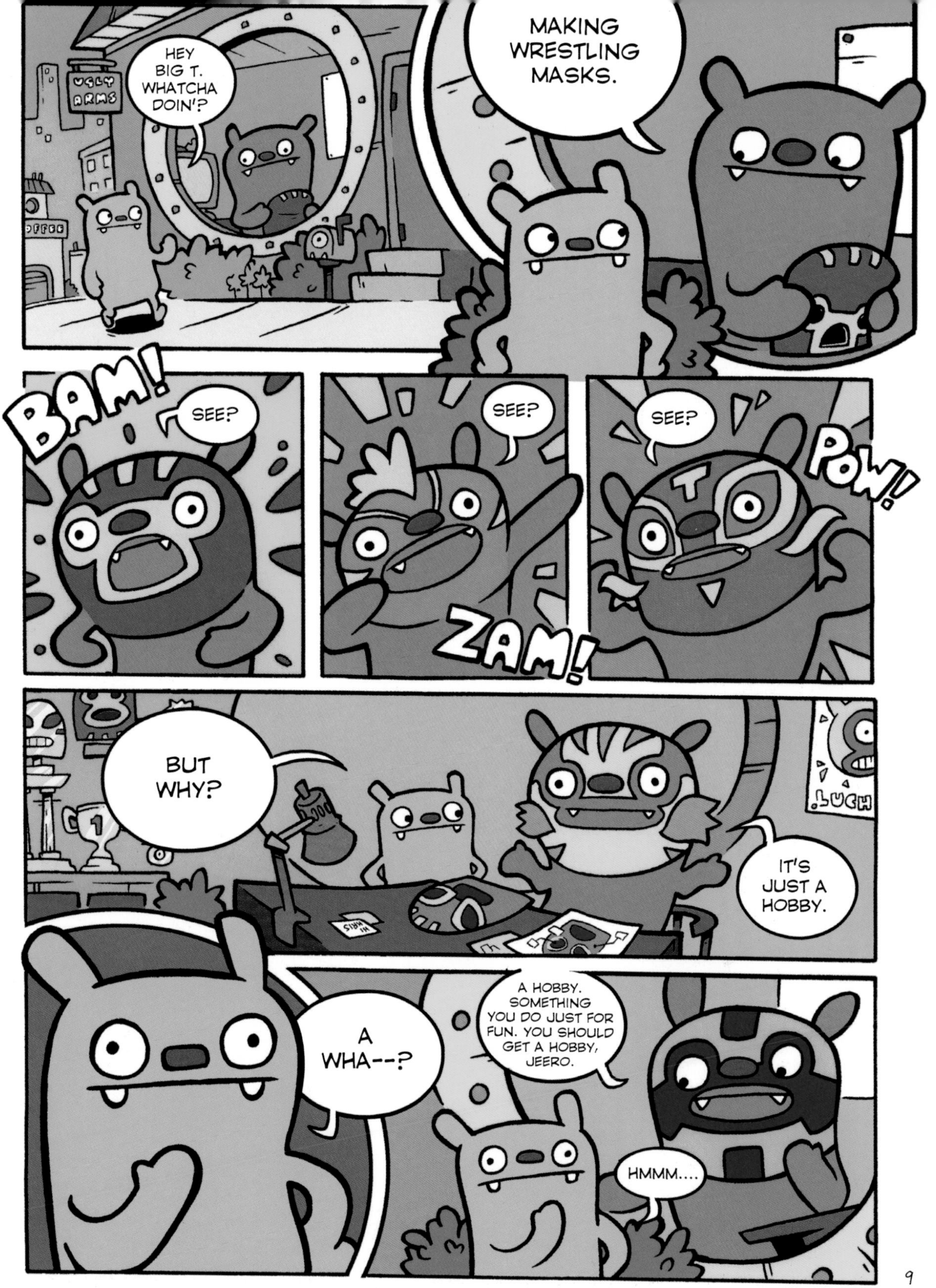
UGLY ARMS
HEY BIG T. WHATCHA DOIN'?
MAKING WRESTLING MASKS.
BAM!
SEE?
SEE?
SEE?
POW!
ZAM!
BUT WHY?
LUCH
IT'S JUST A HOBBY.
A WHA--?
A HOBBY. SOMETHING YOU DO JUST FOR FUN. YOU SHOULD GET A HOBBY, JEERO.
HMMM....

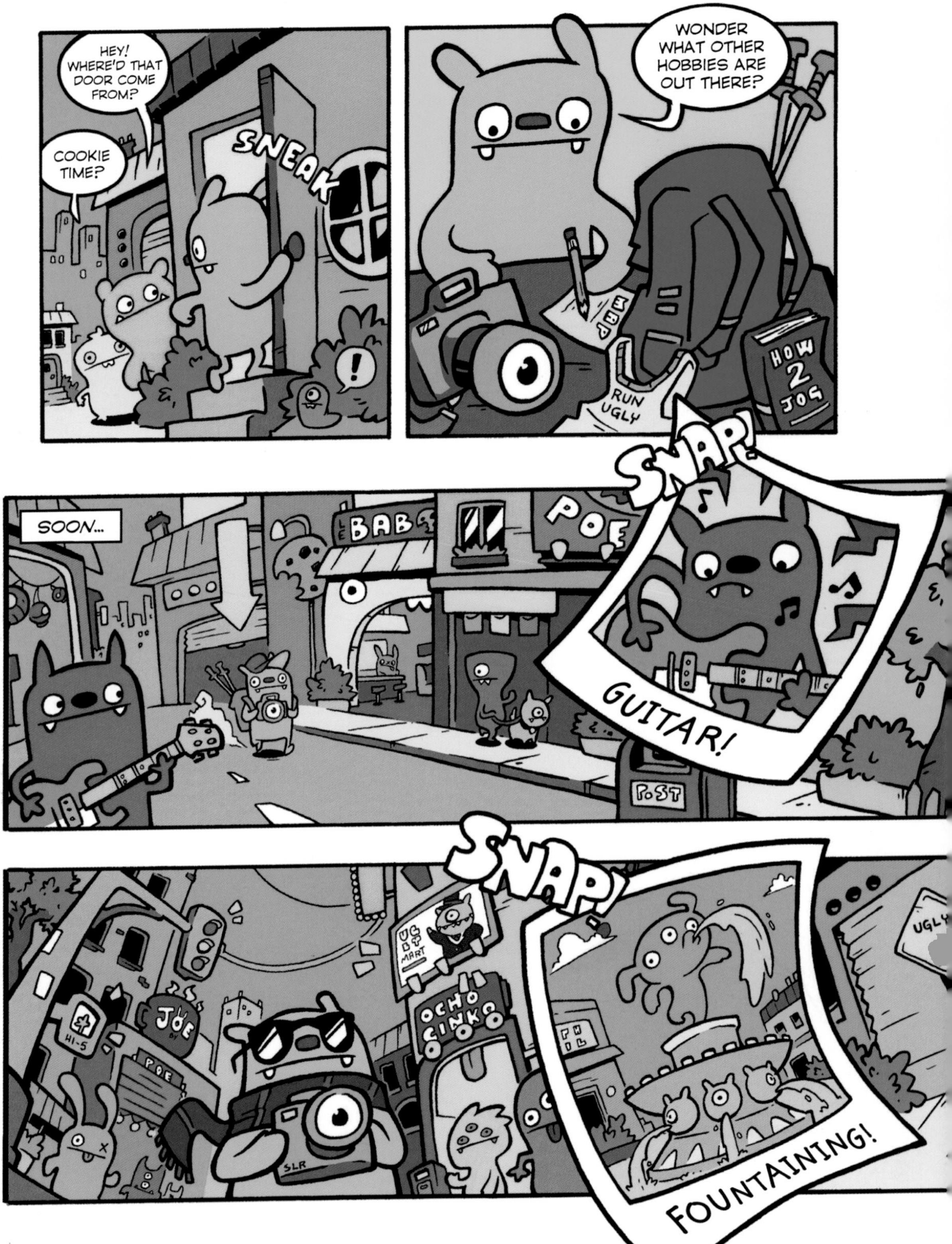
HEY! WHERE'D THAT DOOR COME FROM?
COOKIE TIME?
SNEAK
!
WONDER WHAT OTHER HOBBIES ARE OUT THERE?
MAP
RUN UGLY
HOW 2 JOG
SNAP!
SOON...
BAB
POE
GUITAR!
POST
SNAP!
FOUNTAINING!
UG BT MART
OCHO CINKO
JOE
HI-5
POE
SLR
UGLY

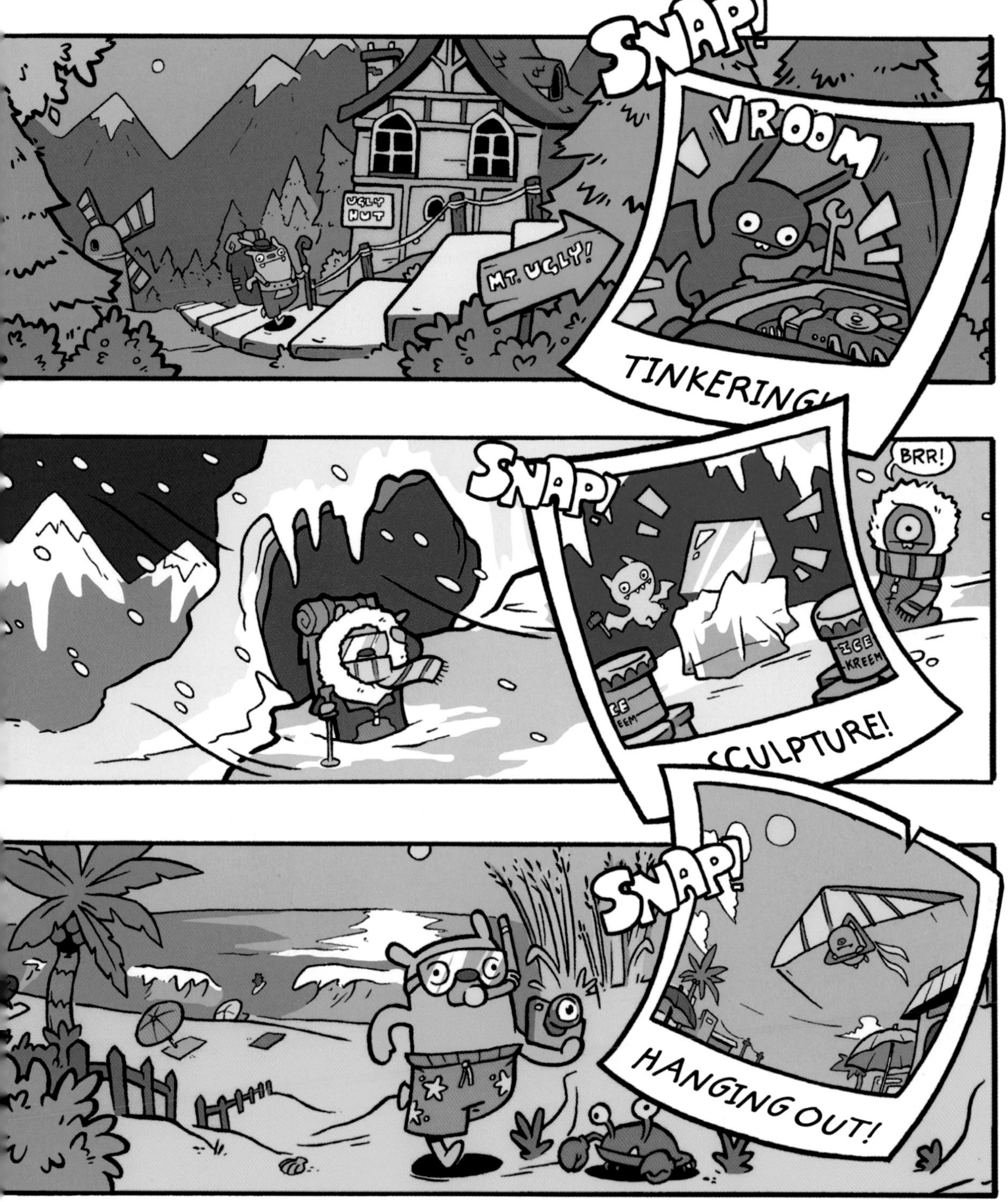
UGLY HUT
MT. UGLY!
SNAP!
VROOM
TINKERING
SNAP!
ICE KREEM
SCULPTURE!
BRR!
SNAP!
HANGING OUT!

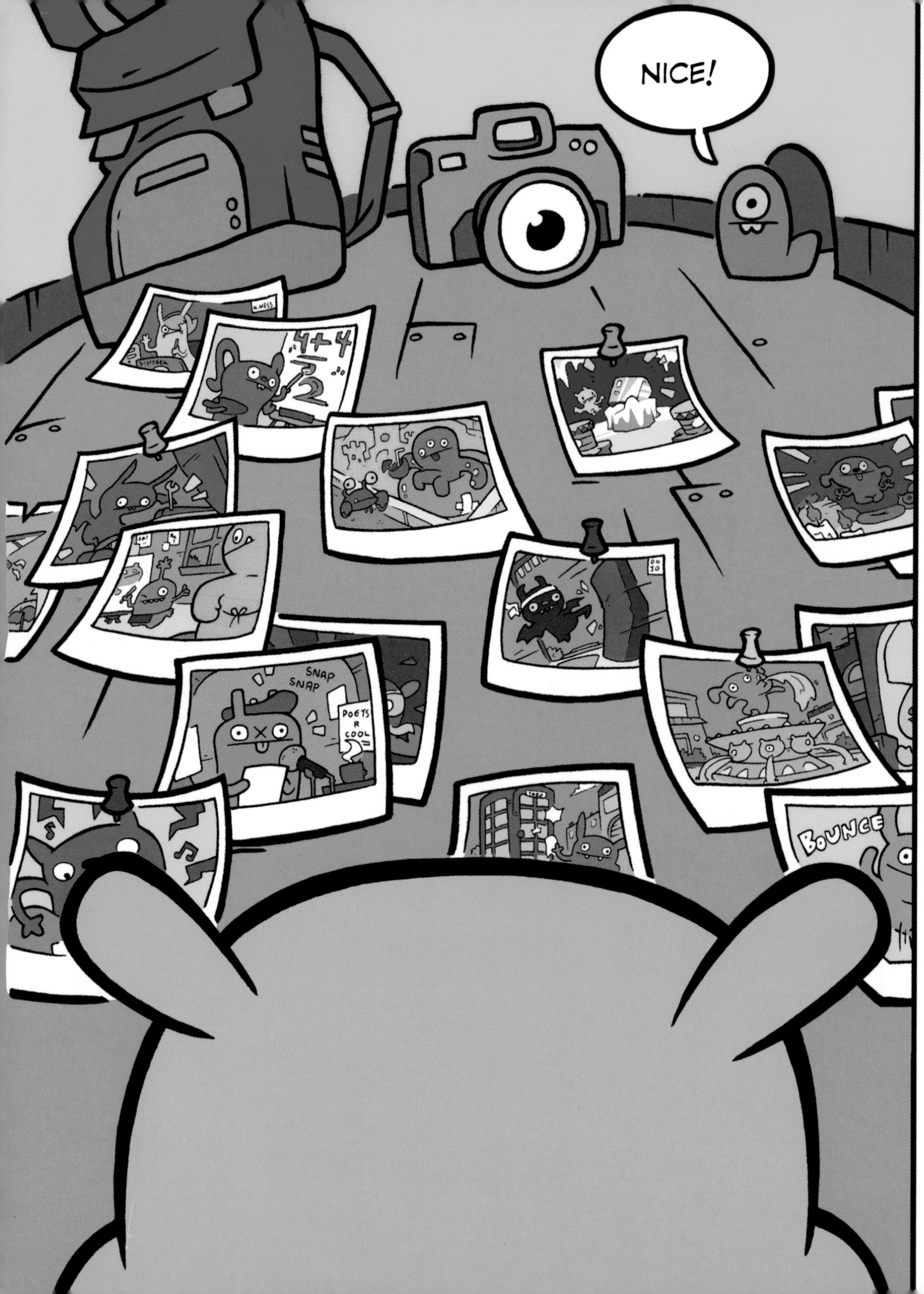
NICE!
SNAP
SNAP
POETS
R
COOL
BOUNCE

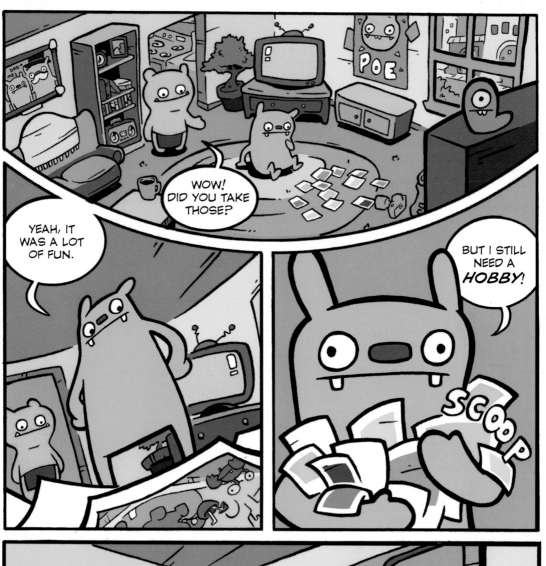

WOW! DID YOU TAKE THOSE?

YEAH, IT WAS A LOT OF FUN.

BUT I STILL NEED A *HOBBY*!

SCOOP

CAN I HAVE A COOKIE NOW?

TOSS

END!

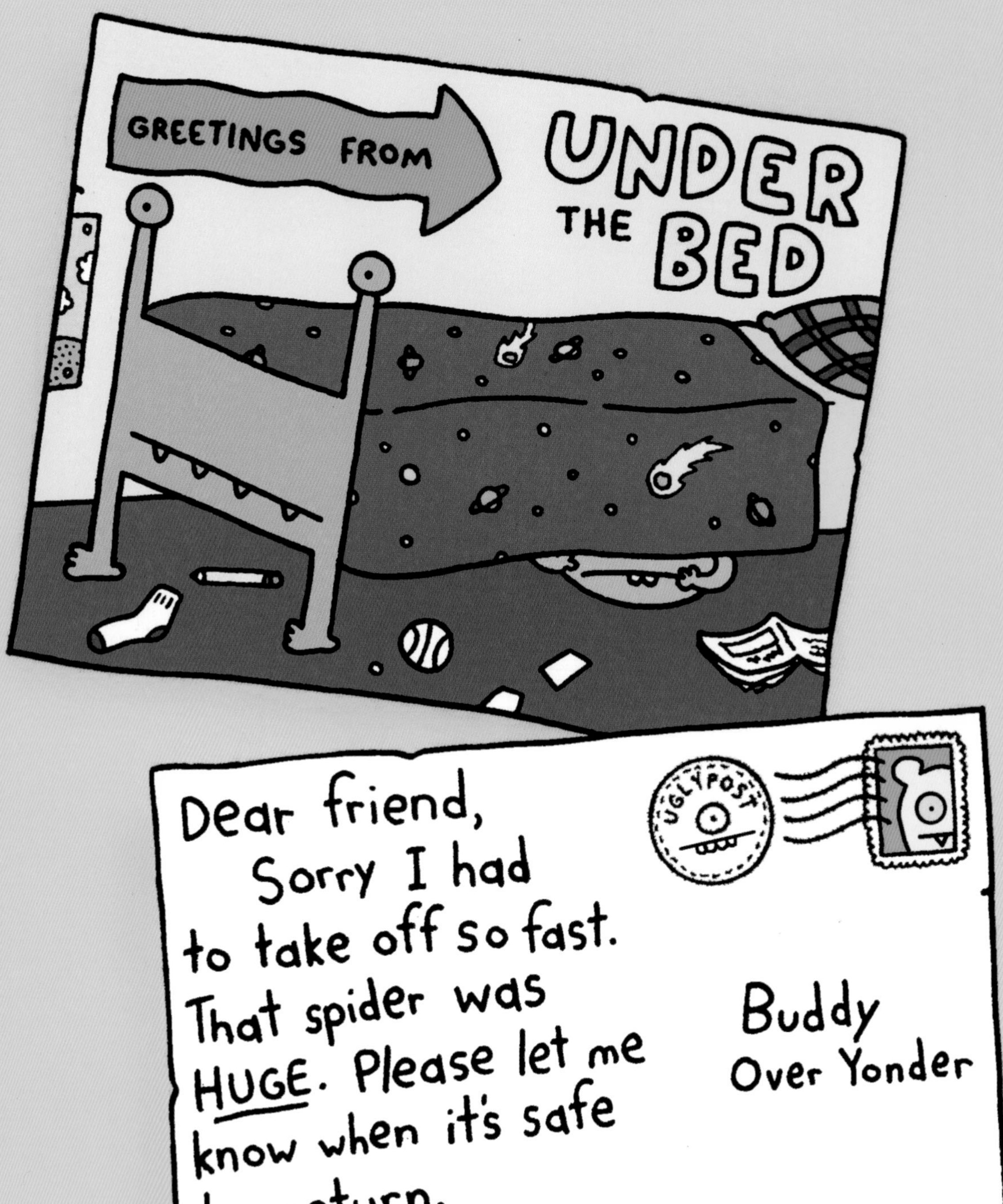
GREETINGS FROM
UNDER THE BED
UGLYPOST
Dear friend,
Sorry I had to take off so fast. That spider was HUGE. Please let me know when it's safe to return.
Love,
Babo
Buddy
Over Yonder

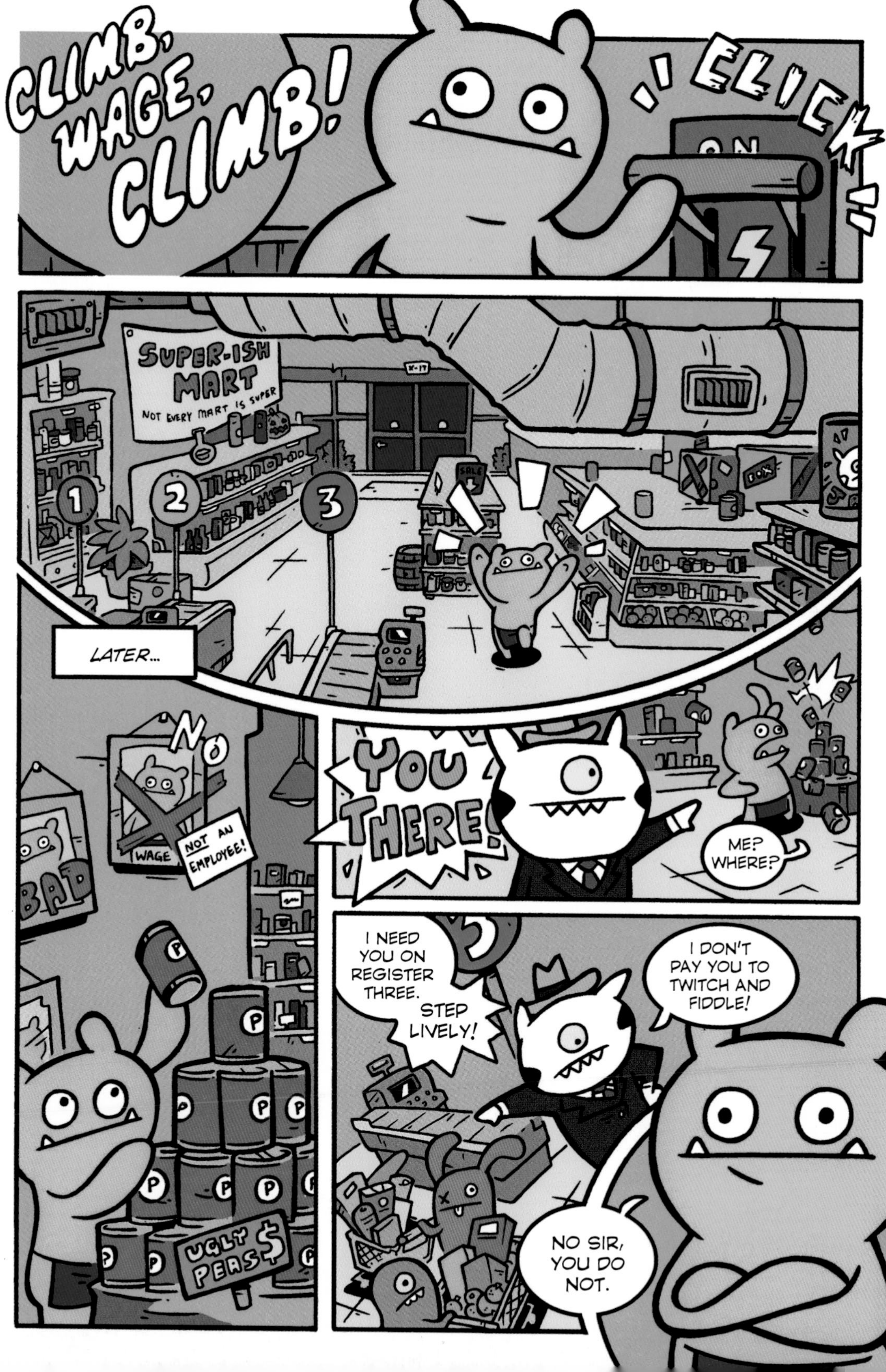
CLIMB, WAGE, CLIMB!
CLICK
ON
SUPER-ISH MART
NOT EVERY MART IS SUPER
1
2
3
SALE
LATER...
NO
WAGE
NOT AN EMPLOYEE!
BAD
YOU THERE!
ME? WHERE?
UGLY PEAS $
I NEED YOU ON REGISTER THREE.
STEP LIVELY!
I DON'T PAY YOU TO TWITCH AND FIDDLE!
NO SIR, YOU DO NOT.

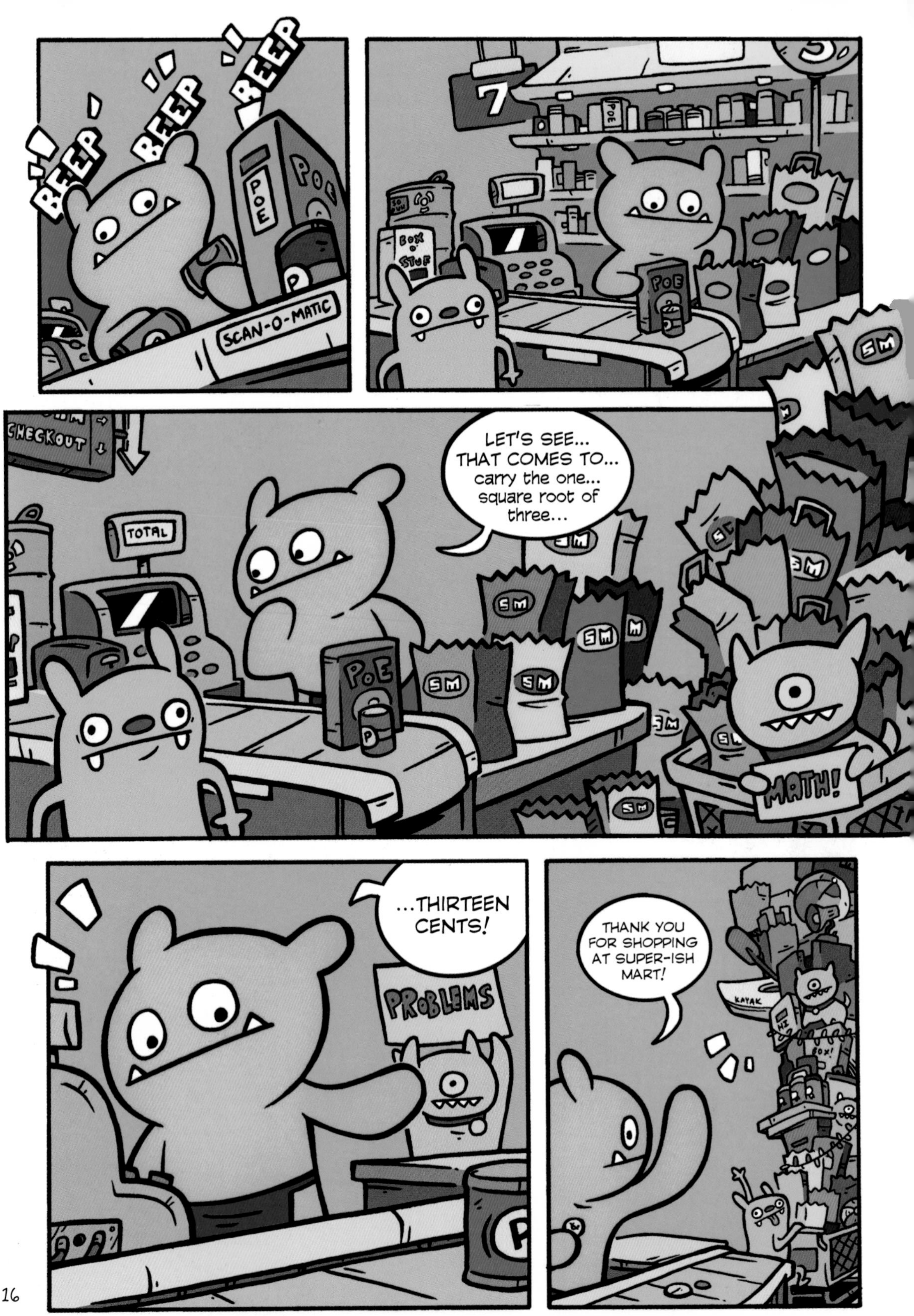
BEEP
BEEP
BEEP
POE
POE
SCAN-O-MATIC
7
POE
BOX O' STUF
POE
CHECKOUT
TOTAL
LET'S SEE... THAT COMES TO... carry the one... square root of three...
PoE
SM
MATH!
...THIRTEEN CENTS!
PROBLEMS
THANK YOU FOR SHOPPING AT SUPER-ISH MART!
KAYAK

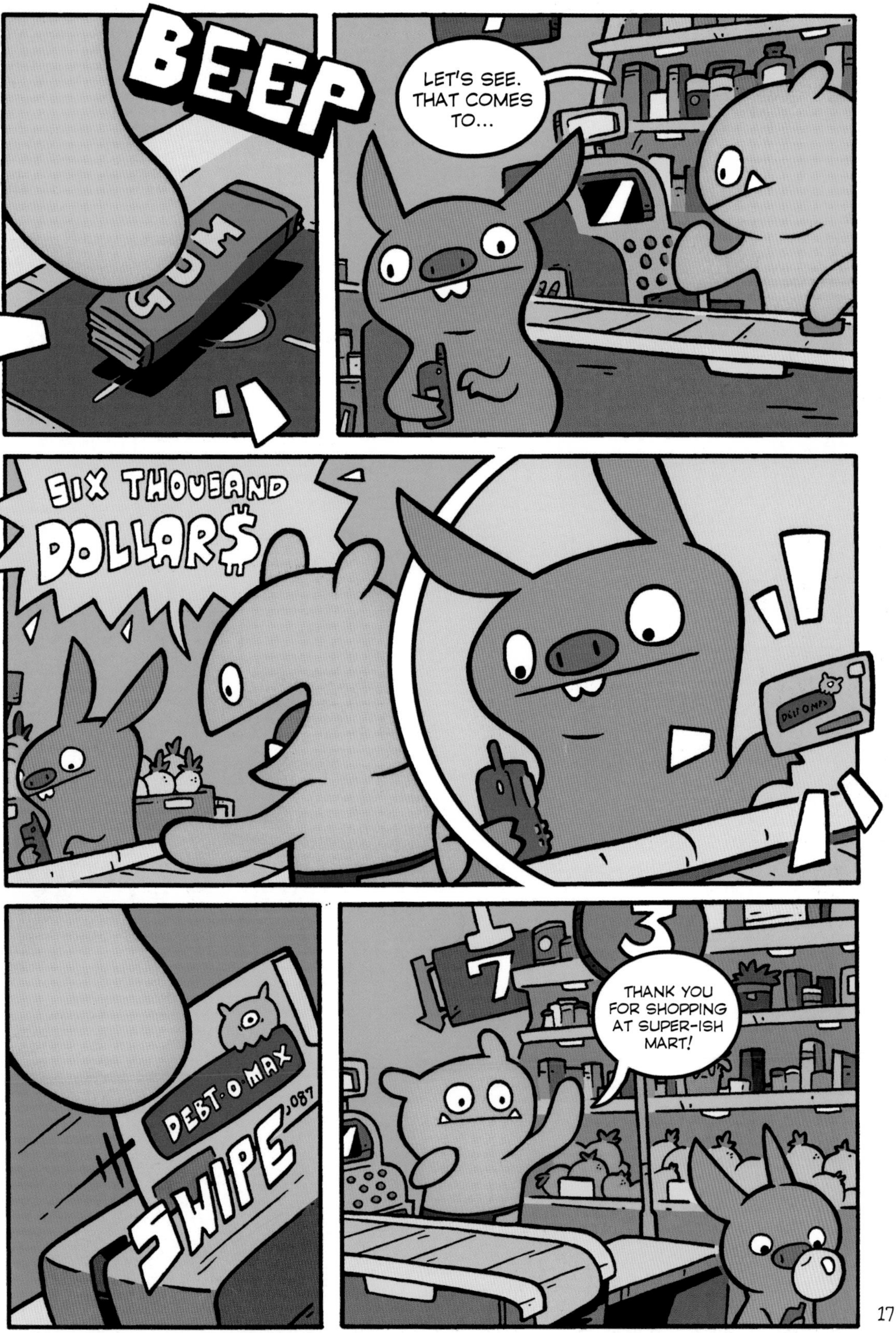
BEEP
GUM
LET'S SEE. THAT COMES TO...
SIX THOUSAND DOLLAR$
DEBT-O-MAX
SWIPE
7
3
THANK YOU FOR SHOPPING AT SUPER-ISH MART!

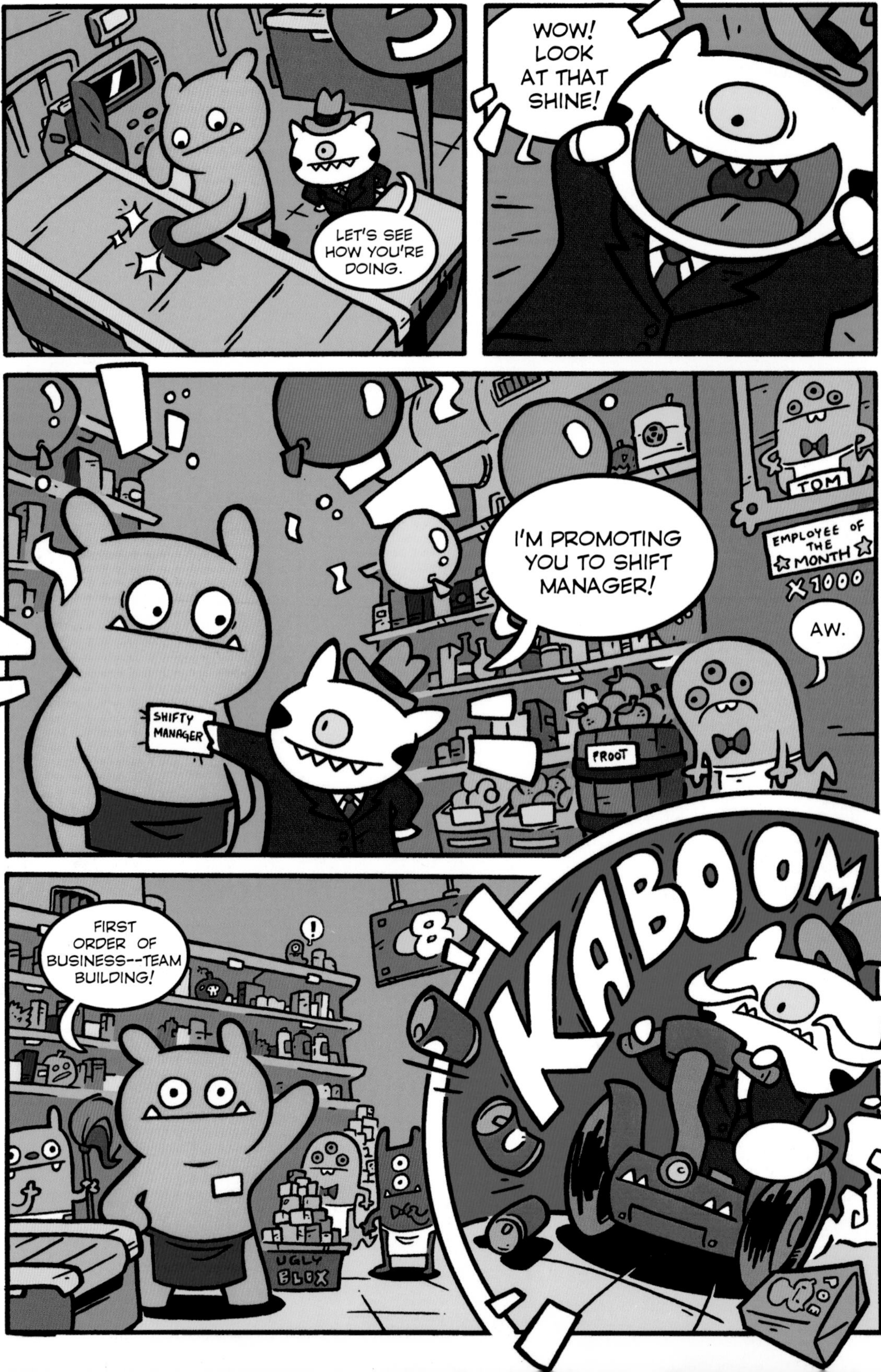
LET'S SEE HOW YOU'RE DOING.
WOW! LOOK AT THAT SHINE!
TOM
EMPLOYEE OF THE MONTH
X1000
I'M PROMOTING YOU TO SHIFT MANAGER!
AW.
SHIFTY MANAGER
FROOT
FIRST ORDER OF BUSINESS--TEAM BUILDING!
UGLY BLOX
KABOOM

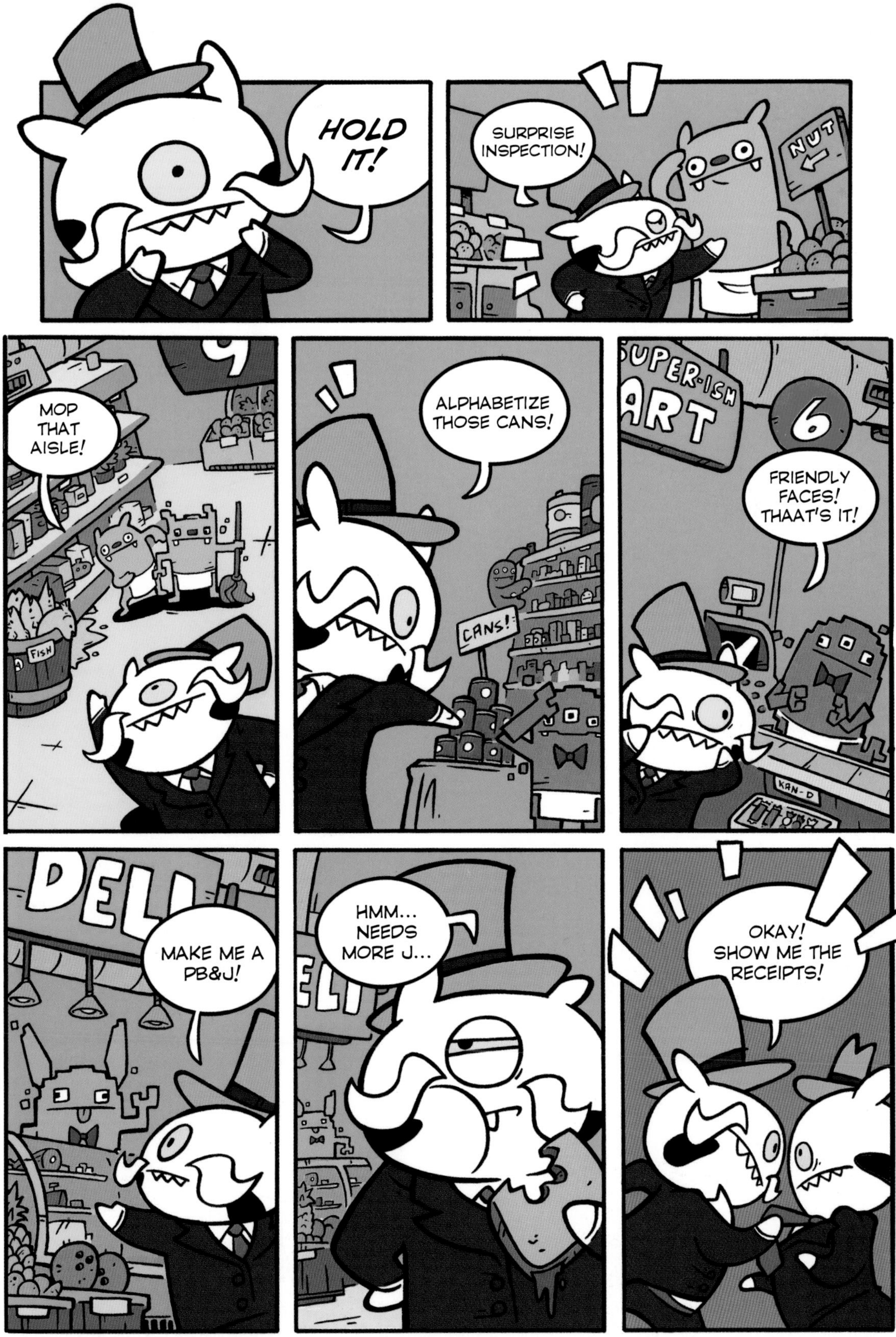
HOLD IT!
SURPRISE INSPECTION!
NUT
MOP THAT AISLE!
FISH
ALPHABETIZE THOSE CANS!
CANS!
SUPER-ISH ART
6
FRIENDLY FACES! THAAT'S IT!
KAN-D
DELI
MAKE ME A PB&J!
HMM... NEEDS MORE J...
OKAY! SHOW ME THE RECEIPTS!

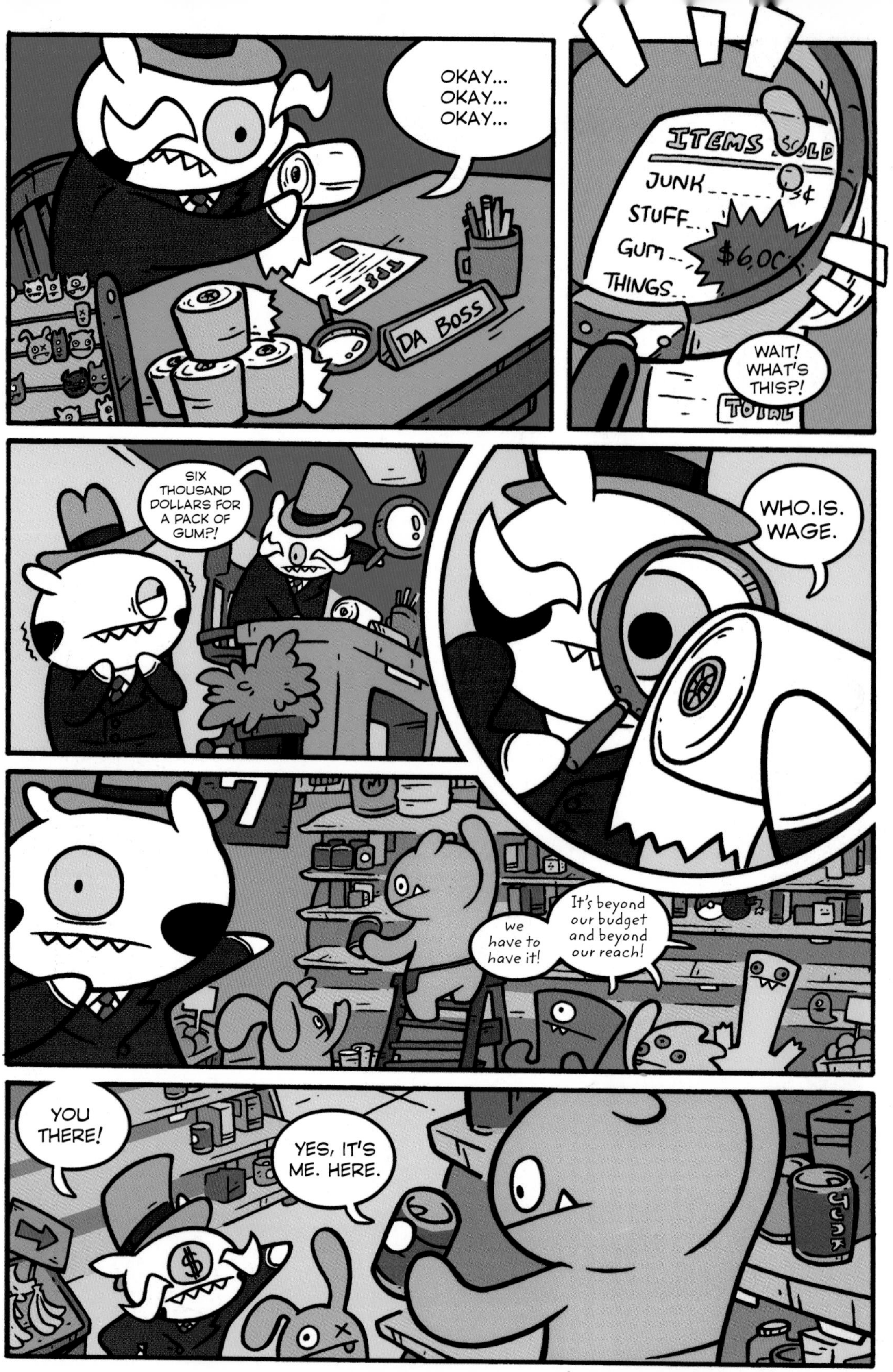

OKAY... OKAY... OKAY...
DA BOSS
ITEMS SOLD
JUNK 13¢
STUFF
GUM $6,00
THINGS
TOTAL
WAIT! WHAT'S THIS?!
SIX THOUSAND DOLLARS FOR A PACK OF GUM?!
WHO.IS. WAGE.
we have to have it!
It's beyond our budget and beyond our reach!
YOU THERE!
YES, IT'S ME. HERE.
JUNK

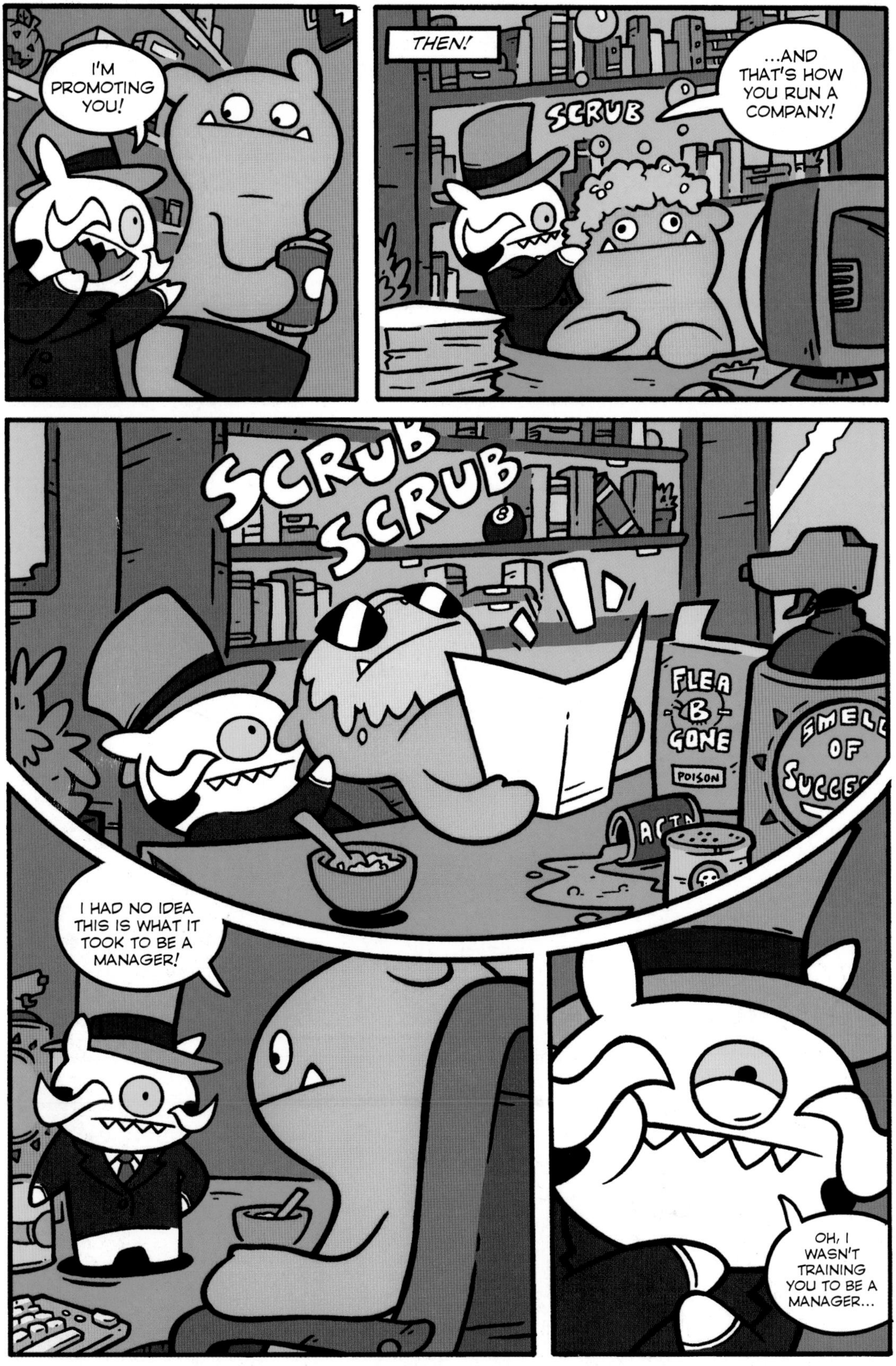
I'M PROMOTING YOU!
THEN!
...AND THAT'S HOW YOU RUN A COMPANY!
SCRUB
SCRUB SCRUB
FLEA -B- GONE
POISON
SMELL OF SUCCE
I HAD NO IDEA THIS IS WHAT IT TOOK TO BE A MANAGER!
OH, I WASN'T TRAINING YOU TO BE A MANAGER...

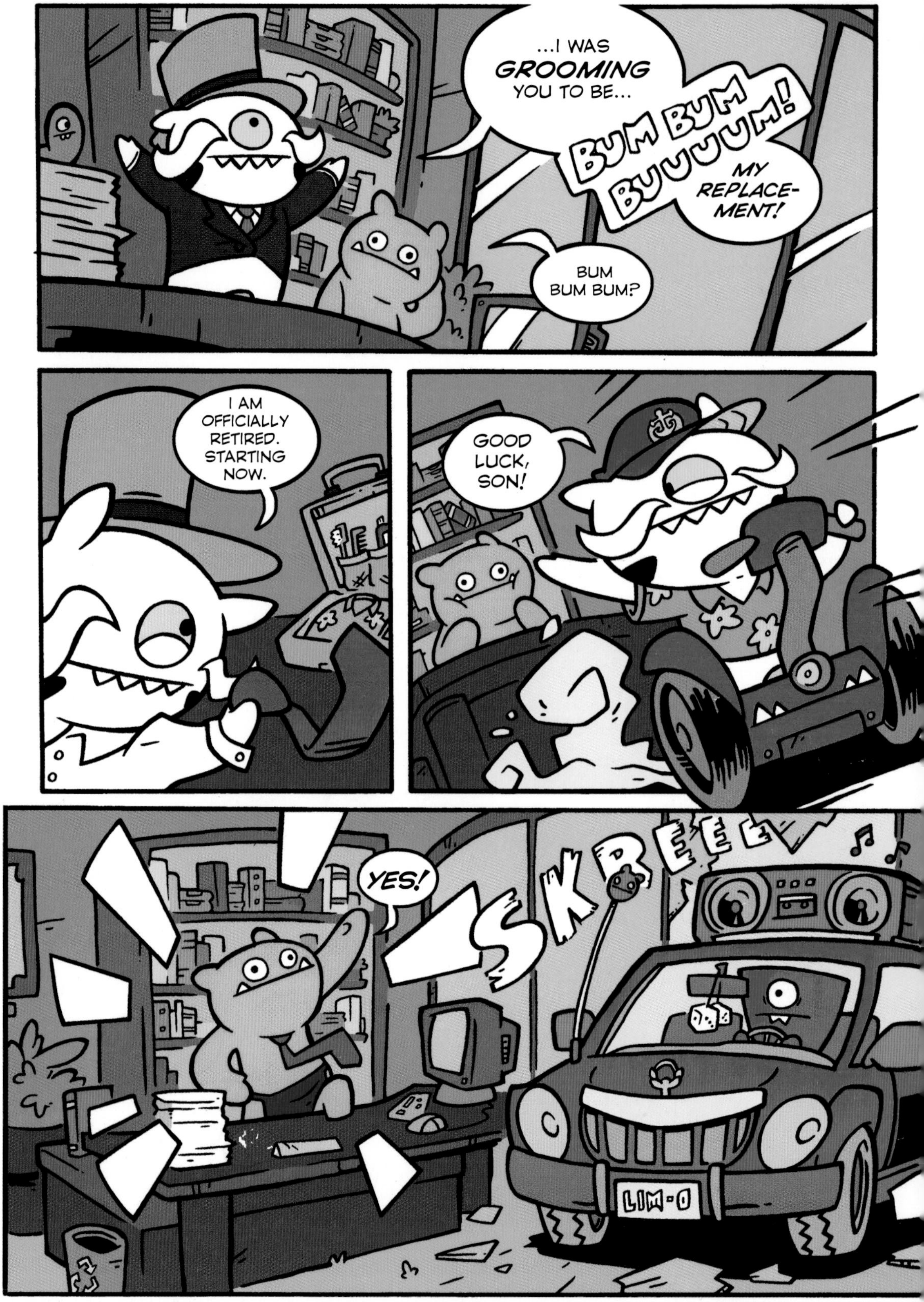
...I WAS *GROOMING* YOU TO BE...
BUM BUM BUUUUM!
MY REPLACEMENT!
BUM BUM BUM?
I AM OFFICIALLY RETIRED. STARTING NOW.
GOOD LUCK, SON!
YES!
SKREEE
LIM-O

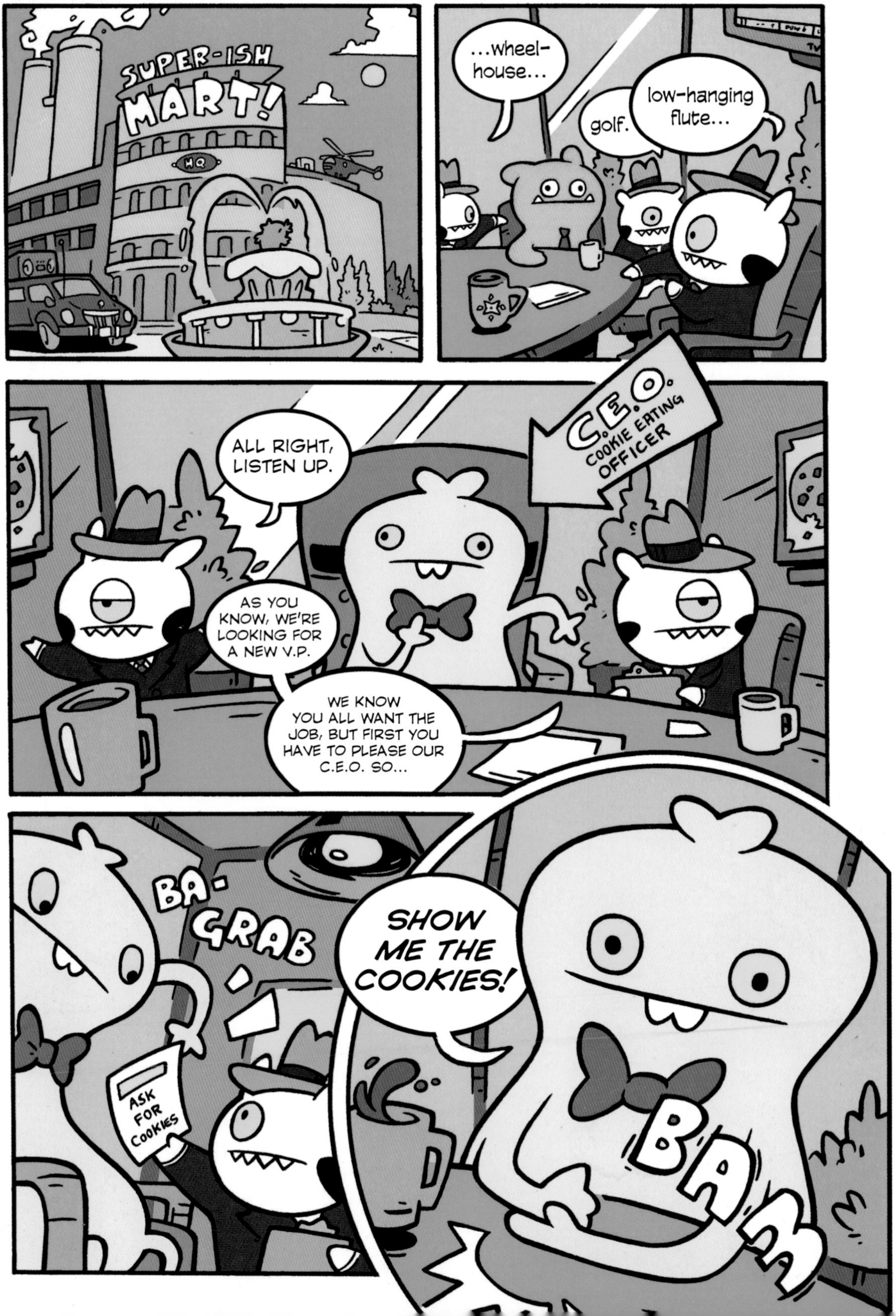
SUPER-ISH
MART!
HQ
...wheel-house...
golf.
low-hanging flute...
ALL RIGHT, LISTEN UP.
C.E.O. COOKIE EATING OFFICER
AS YOU KNOW, WE'RE LOOKING FOR A NEW V.P.
WE KNOW YOU ALL WANT THE JOB, BUT FIRST YOU HAVE TO PLEASE OUR C.E.O. SO...
BA-GRAB
ASK FOR COOKIES
SHOW ME THE COOKIES!
BAM

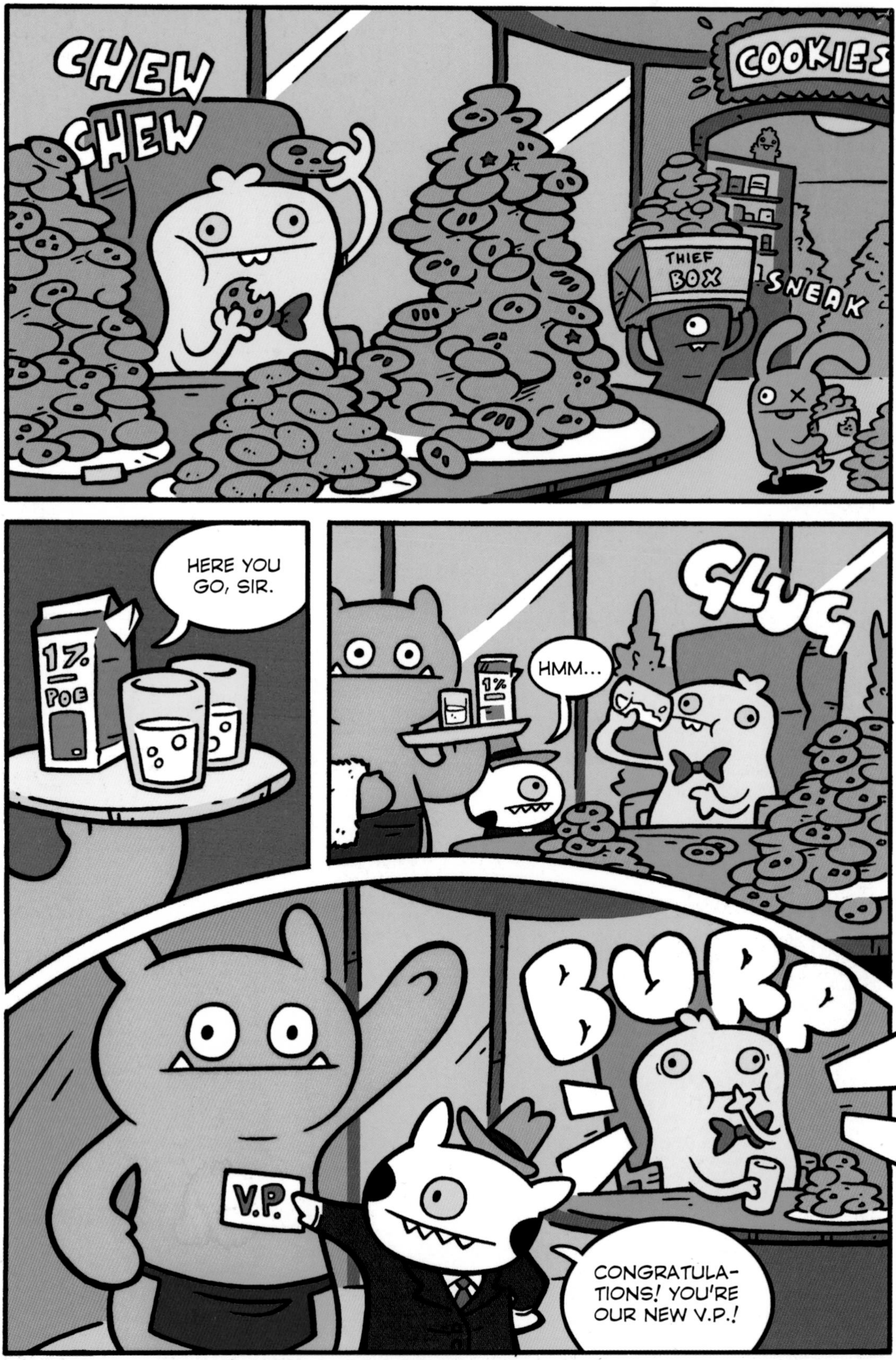
CHEW CHEW
COOKIES
THIEF BOX
SNEAK
HERE YOU GO, SIR.
1% POE
GLUG
HMM...
1%
BURP
V.P.
CONGRATULA-TIONS! YOU'RE OUR NEW V.P.!

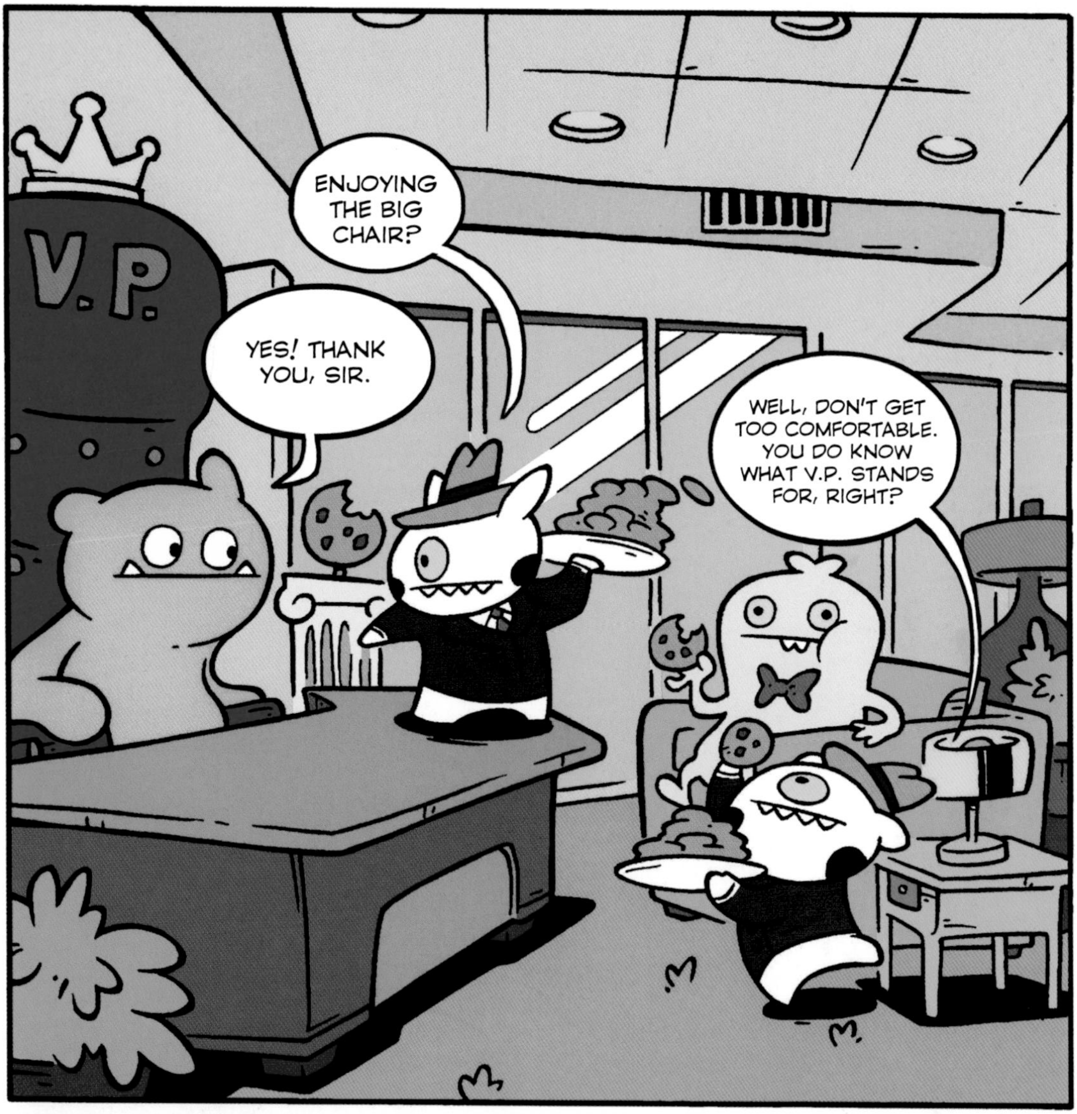
ENJOYING THE BIG CHAIR?
YES! THANK YOU, SIR.
WELL, DON'T GET TOO COMFORTABLE. YOU DO KNOW WHAT V.P. STANDS FOR, RIGHT?

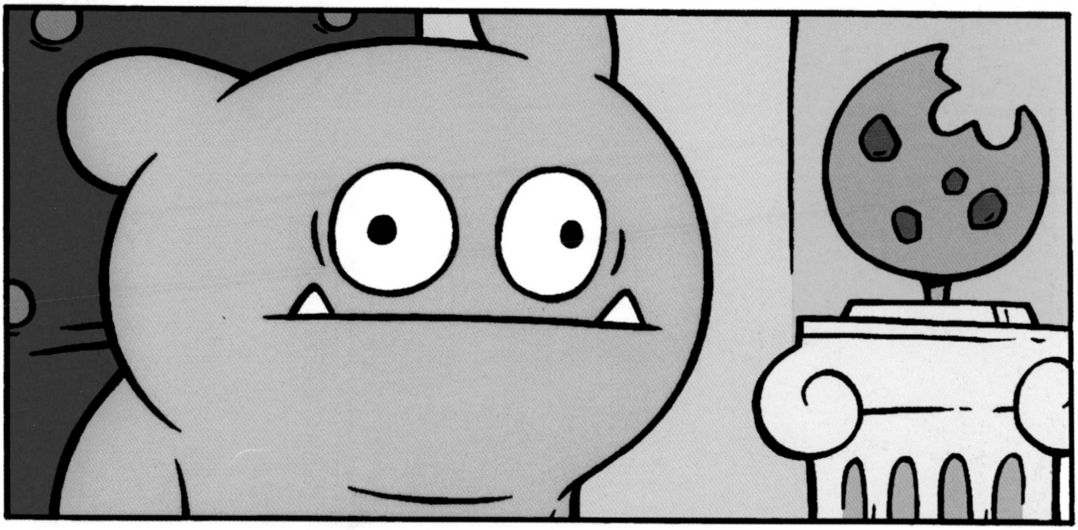

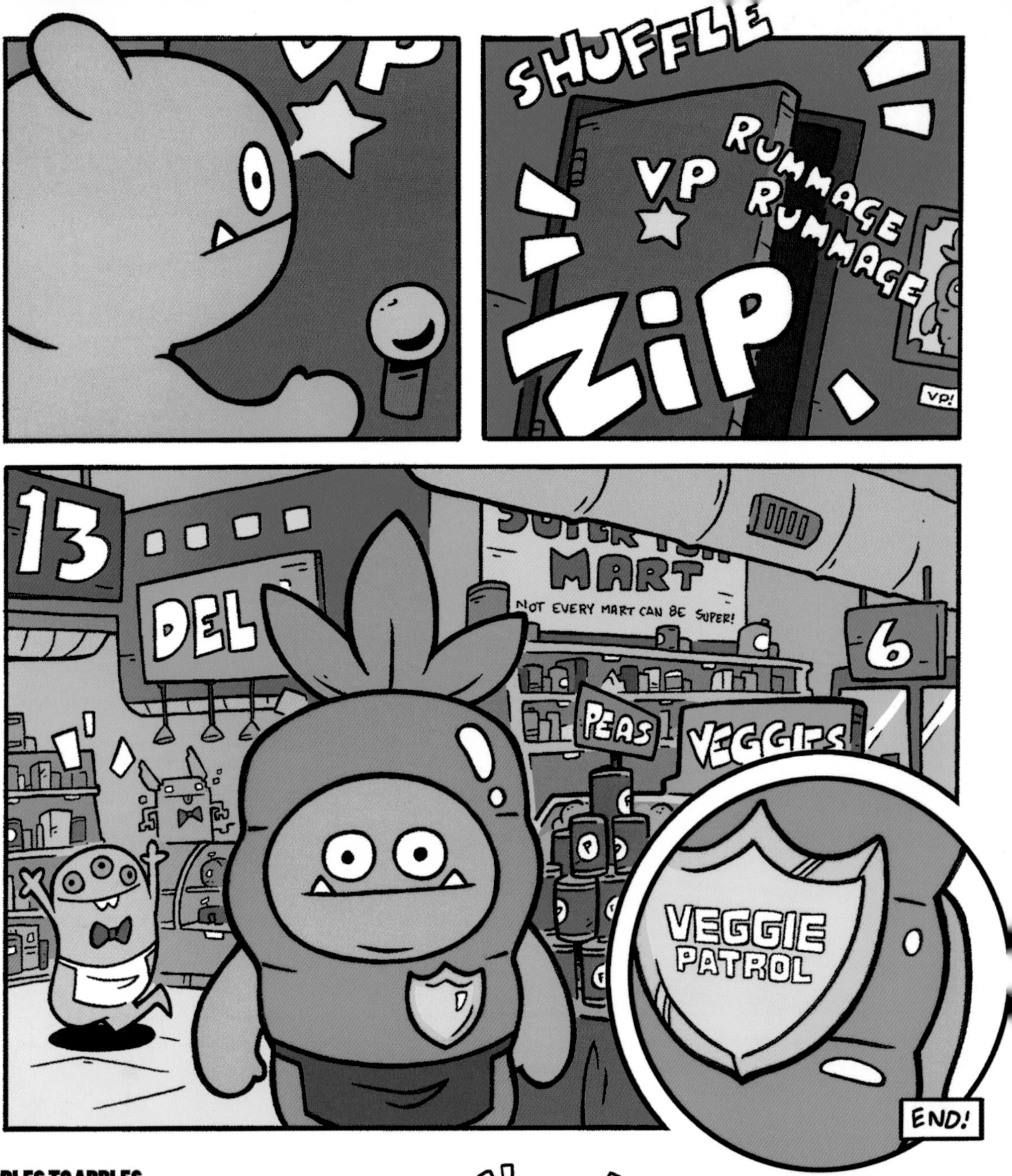
VP
SHUFFLE
VP
RUMMAGE
RUMMAGE
RUMMAGE
ZIP
VP!
13
DEL
MART
NOT EVERY MART CAN BE SUPER!
6
PEAS
VEGGIES
VEGGIE
PATROL
END!

APPLES TO APPLES

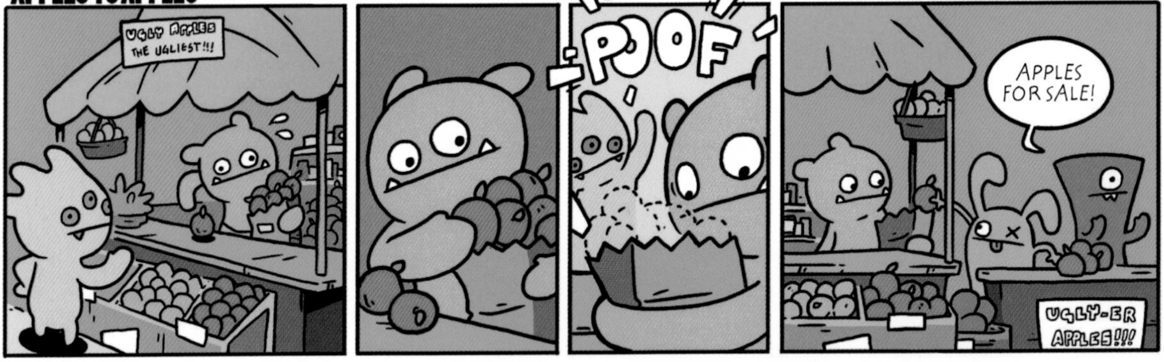
UGLY APPLES
THE UGLIEST!!!
POOF
APPLES FOR SALE!
UGLY-ER APPLES!!!

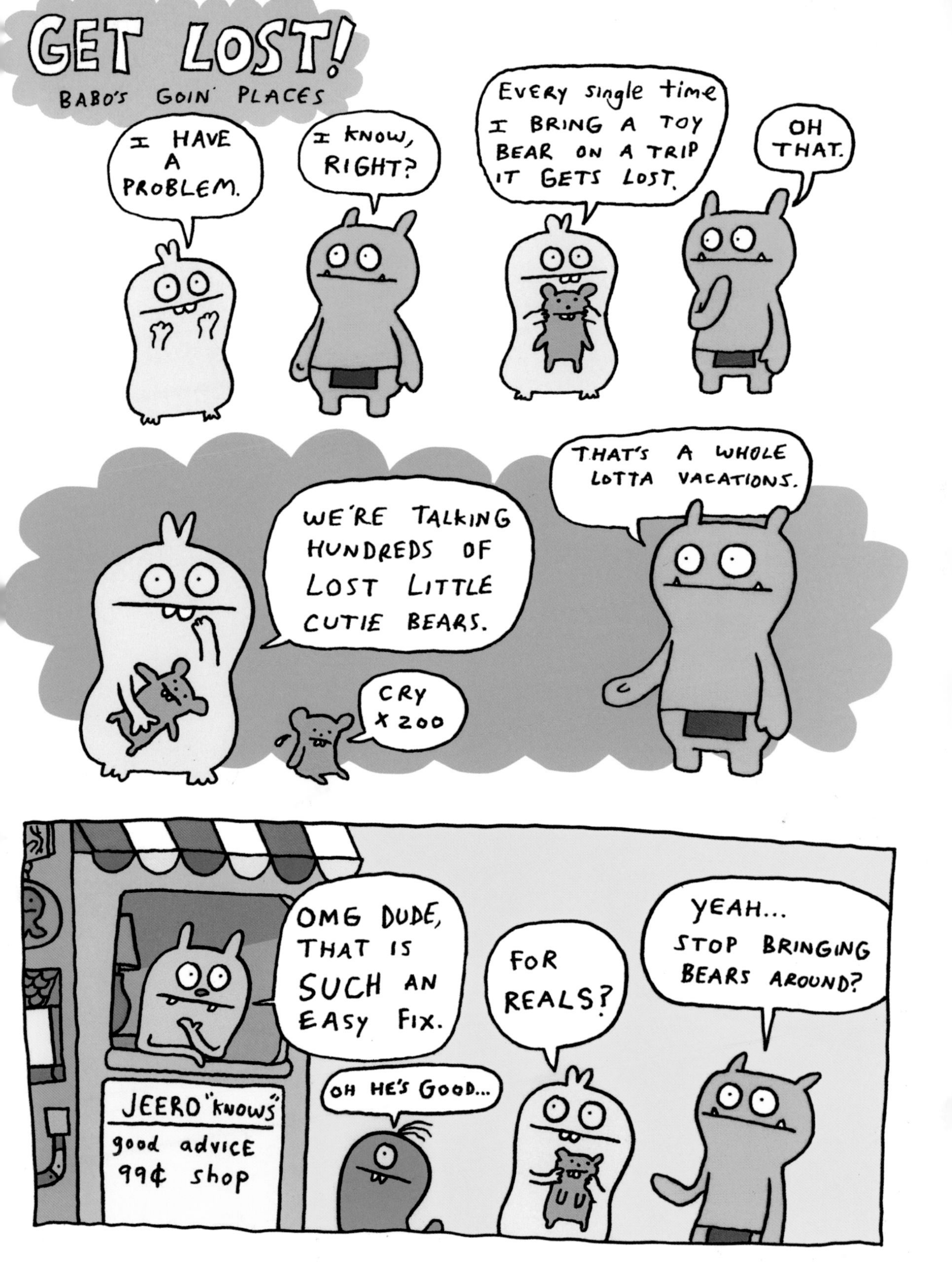
GET LOST!
BABO'S GOIN' PLACES
I HAVE A PROBLEM.
I KNOW, RIGHT?
Every single time I BRING A TOY BEAR ON A TRIP IT GETS LOST.
OH THAT.
WE'RE TALKING HUNDREDS OF LOST LITTLE CUTIE BEARS.
CRY X 200
THAT'S A WHOLE LOTTA VACATIONS.
JEERO "KNOWS"
good advice
99¢ shop
OMG DUDE, THAT IS SUCH AN EASY FIX.
OH HE'S GOOD...
FOR REALS?
YEAH... STOP BRINGING BEARS AROUND?

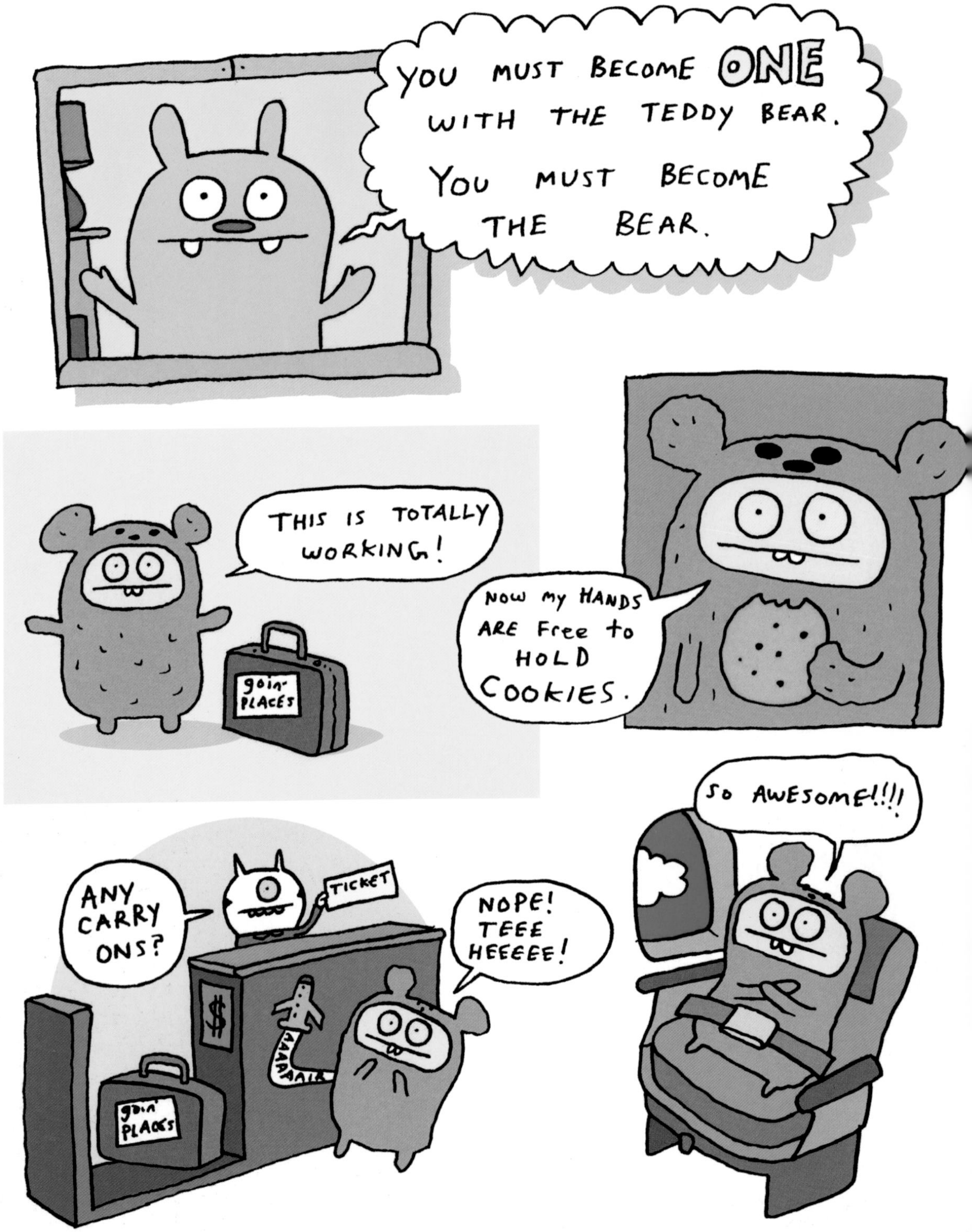
YOU MUST BECOME ONE WITH THE TEDDY BEAR. YOU MUST BECOME THE BEAR.
THIS IS TOTALLY WORKING!
goin' PLACES
NOW MY HANDS ARE FREE TO HOLD COOKIES.
ANY CARRY ONS?
TICKET
NOPE! TEEE HEEEEEE!
$
AAAAAAAIR
goin' PLACES
SO AWESOME!!!!

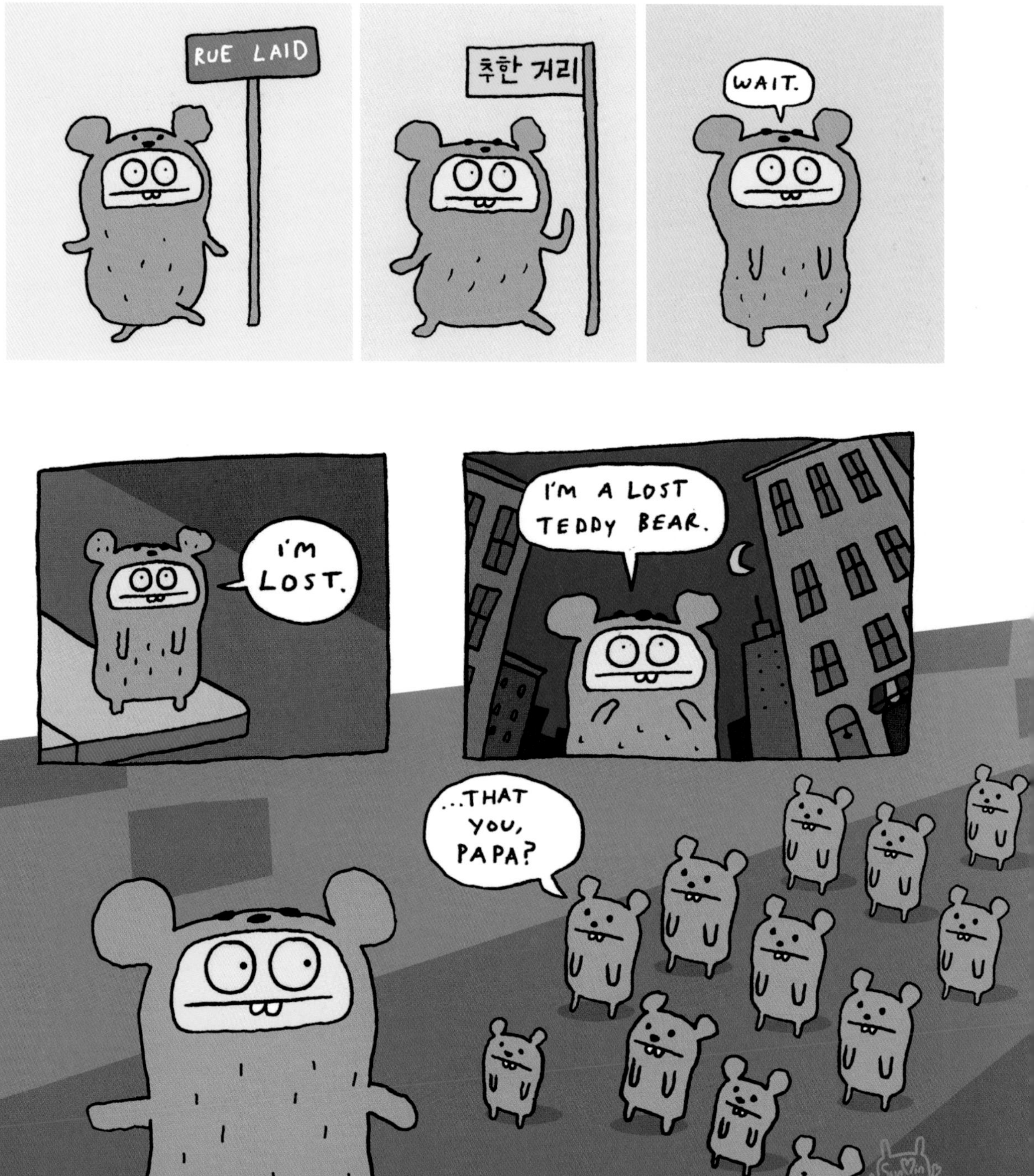
RUE LAID
추한 거리
WAIT.
I'M LOST.
I'M A LOST TEDDY BEAR.
...THAT YOU, PAPA?
SunMin DAVID
the END?

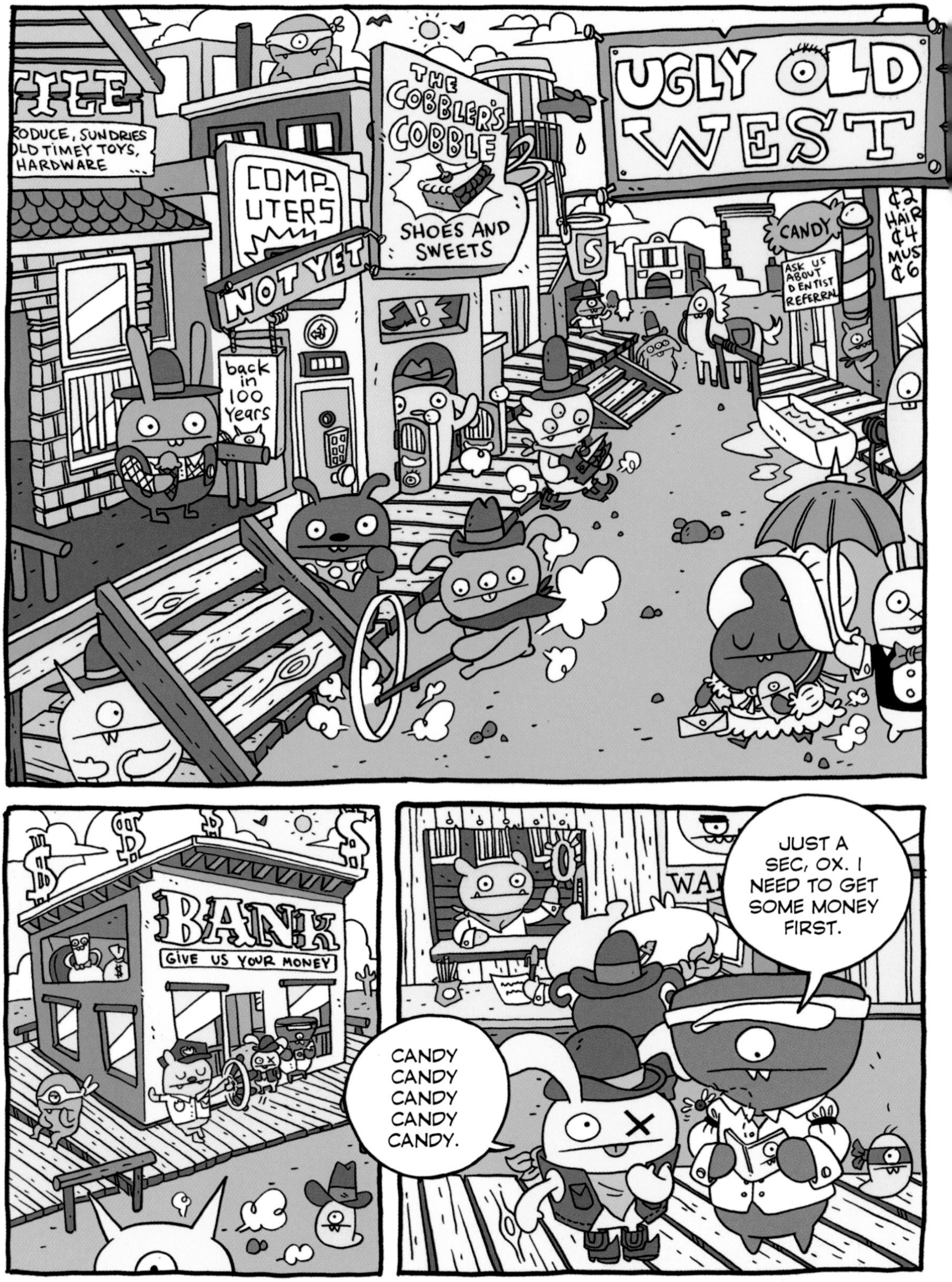
UGLY OLD WEST
THE COBBLER'S COBBLE
SHOES AND SWEETS
COMP-UTERS
NOT YET
back in 100 Years
CANDY
ASK US ABOUT DENTIST REFERRAL
BANK
GIVE US YOUR MONEY
JUST A SEC, OX. I NEED TO GET SOME MONEY FIRST.
CANDY CANDY CANDY CANDY CANDY.

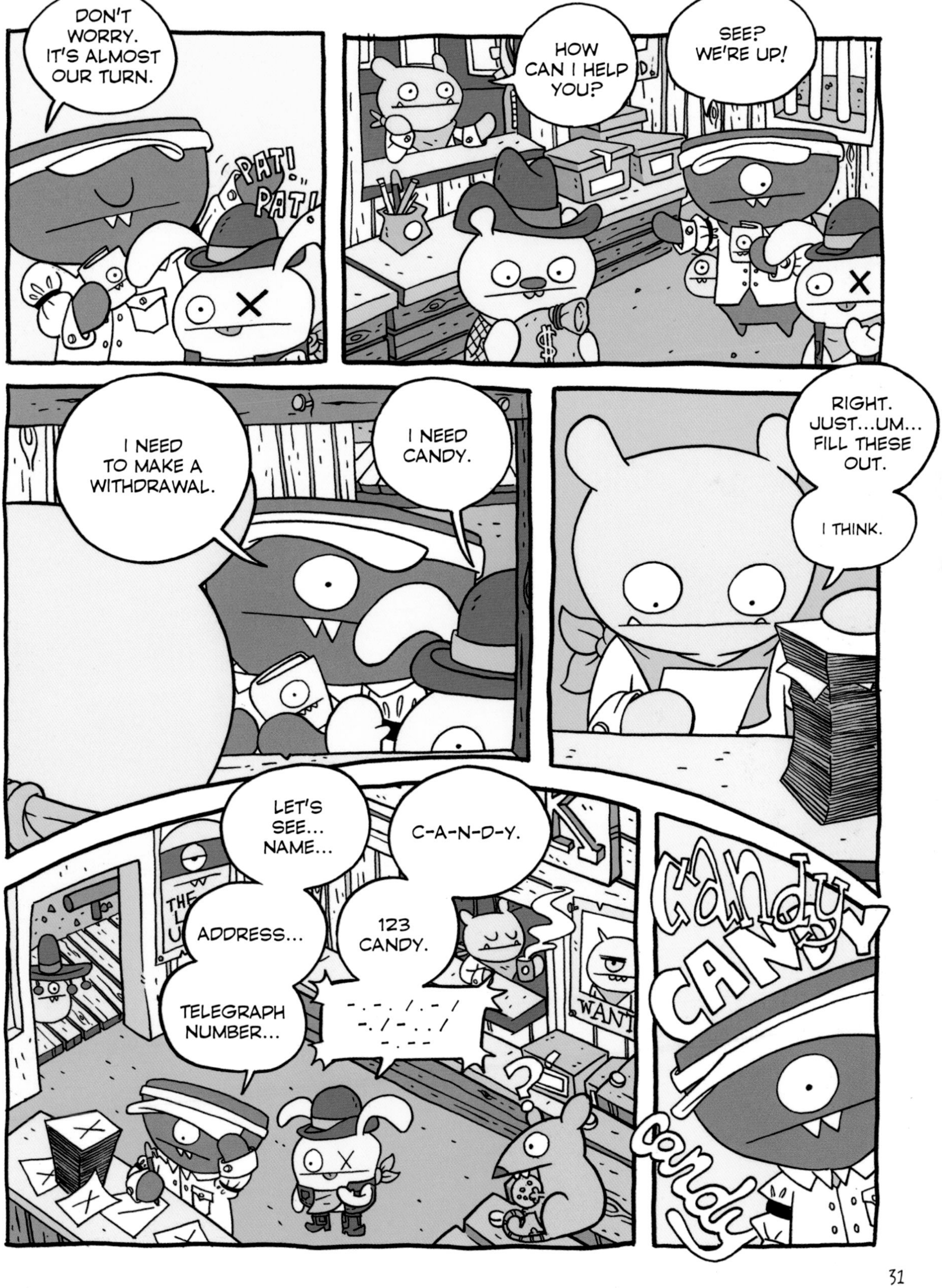
DON'T WORRY. IT'S ALMOST OUR TURN.
PAT! PAT!
HOW CAN I HELP YOU?
SEE? WE'RE UP!
I NEED TO MAKE A WITHDRAWAL.
I NEED CANDY.
RIGHT. JUST...UM... FILL THESE OUT.
I THINK.
LET'S SEE... NAME...
C-A-N-D-Y.
ADDRESS...
123 CANDY.
TELEGRAPH NUMBER...
-.-. .- -. -.. -.--
WANT
candy
CANDY
candy
candy

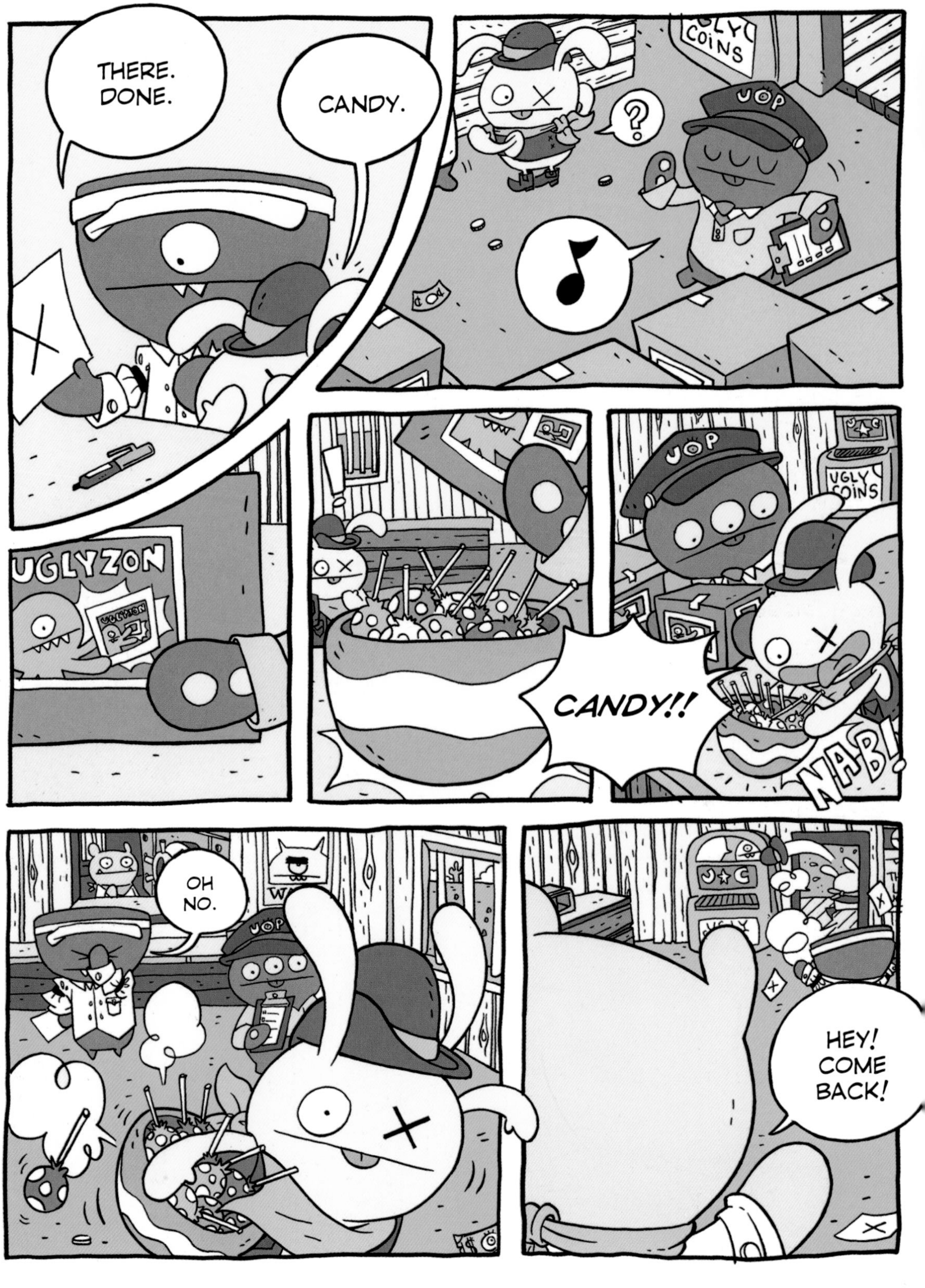
THERE. DONE.
CANDY.
UGLY COINS
UOP
?
UGLYZON
UGLY COINS
UOP
CANDY!!
NAB!
OH NO.
UOP
HEY! COME BACK!

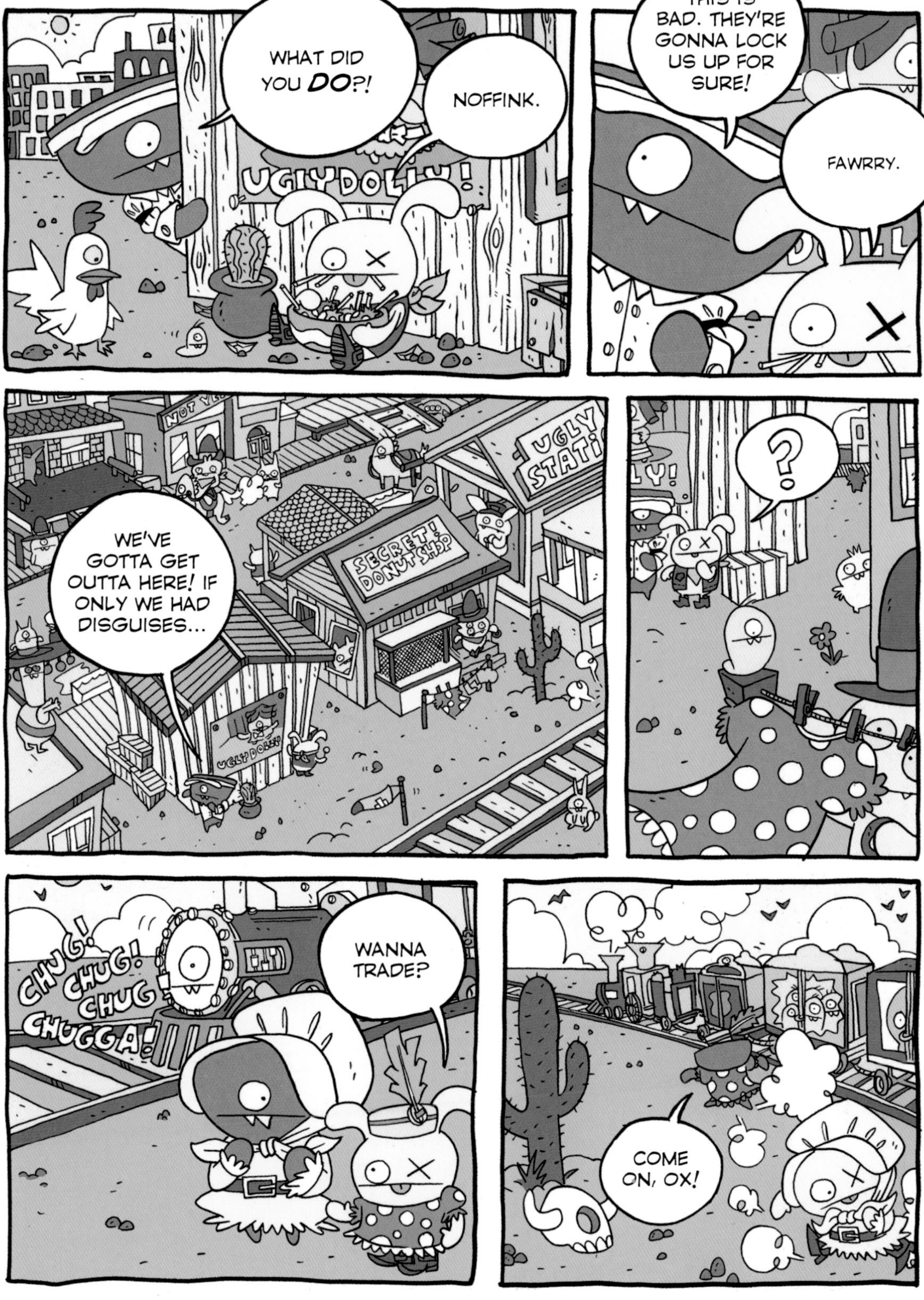

WHAT DID YOU DO?!
NOFFINK.
UGLYDOLLY!
THIS IS BAD. THEY'RE GONNA LOCK US UP FOR SURE!
FAWRRY.
SECRET! DONUT SHOP
UGLY STATI
WE'VE GOTTA GET OUTTA HERE! IF ONLY WE HAD DISGUISES...
?
CHUG! CHUG! CHUG CHUGGA!
WANNA TRADE?
COME ON, OX!

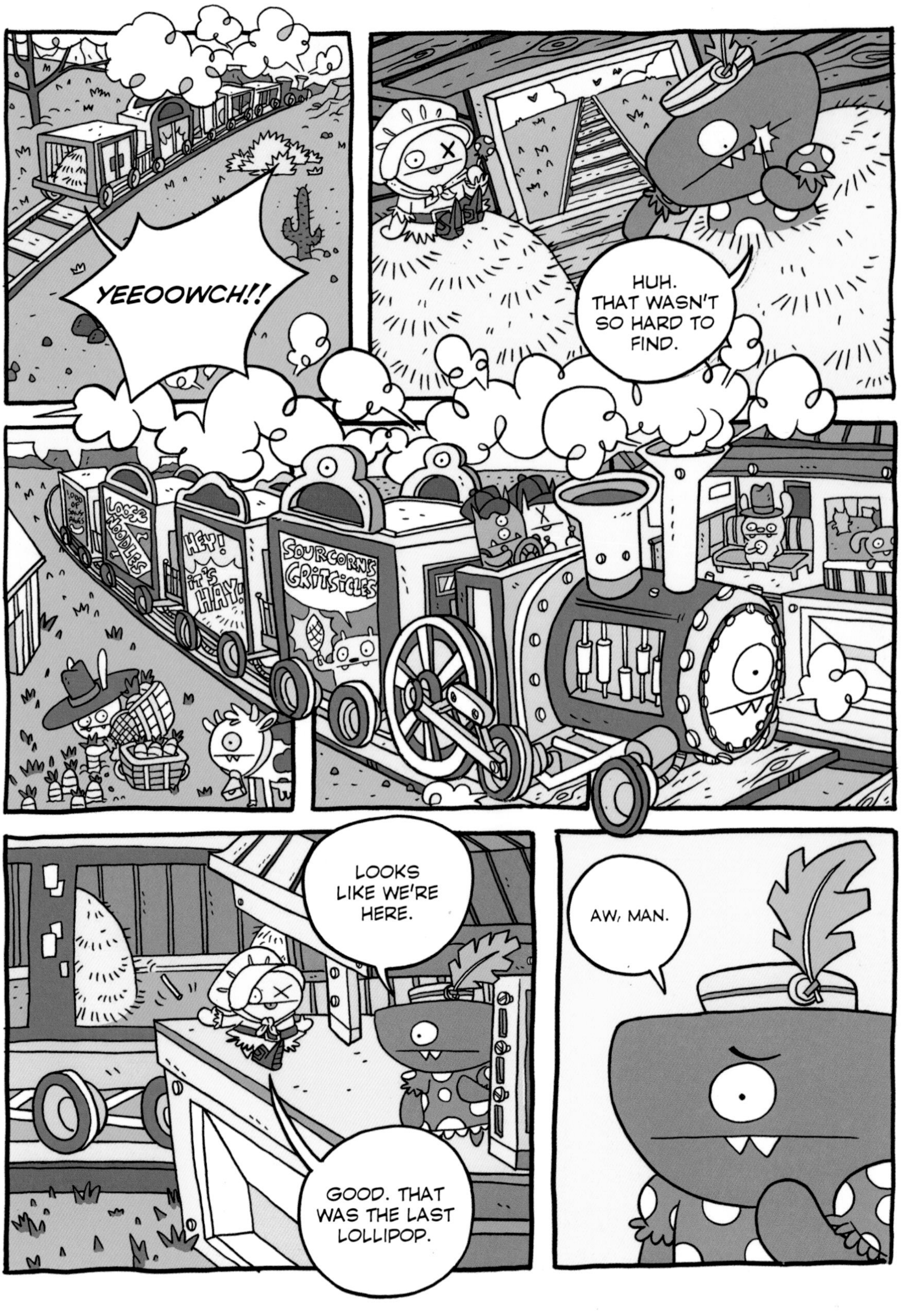
YEEOOWCH!!
HUH. THAT WASN'T SO HARD TO FIND.
LOOSE NOODLES
HEY! it's HAY!
SOURCORN'S GRITSICLES
LOOKS LIKE WE'RE HERE.
GOOD. THAT WAS THE LAST LOLLIPOP.
AW, MAN.

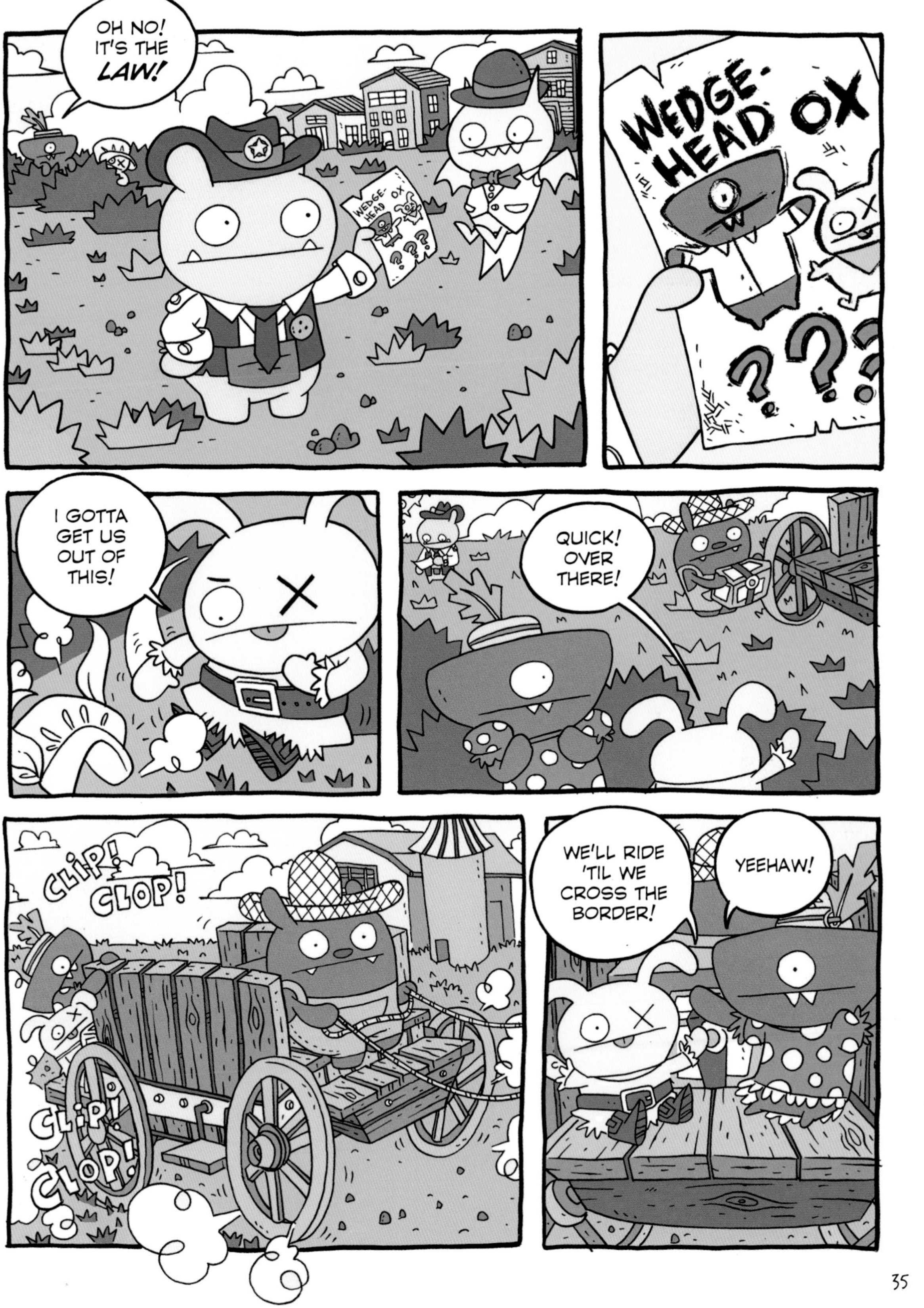
OH NO! IT'S THE LAW!
WEDGE-HEAD OX
WEDGE-HEAD OX
I GOTTA GET US OUT OF THIS!
QUICK! OVER THERE!
CLIP! CLOP!
CLIP! CLOP!
WE'LL RIDE 'TIL WE CROSS THE BORDER!
YEEHAW!

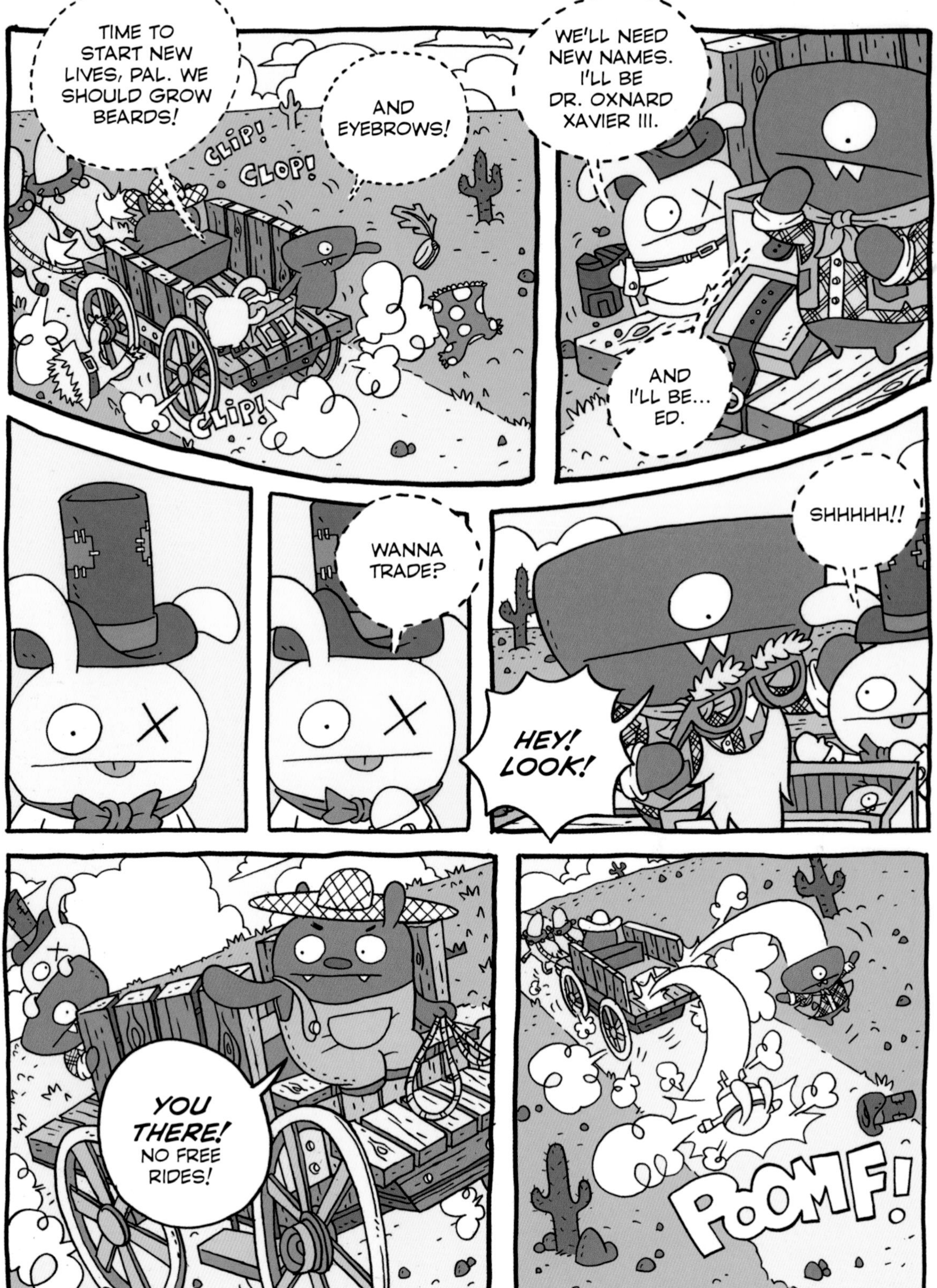

TIME TO START NEW LIVES, PAL. WE SHOULD GROW BEARDS!
CLIP! CLOP!
AND EYEBROWS!
CLIP!
WE'LL NEED NEW NAMES. I'LL BE DR. OXNARD XAVIER III.
AND I'LL BE... ED.
WANNA TRADE?
SHHHHH!!
HEY! LOOK!
YOU THERE! NO FREE RIDES!
POOMF!

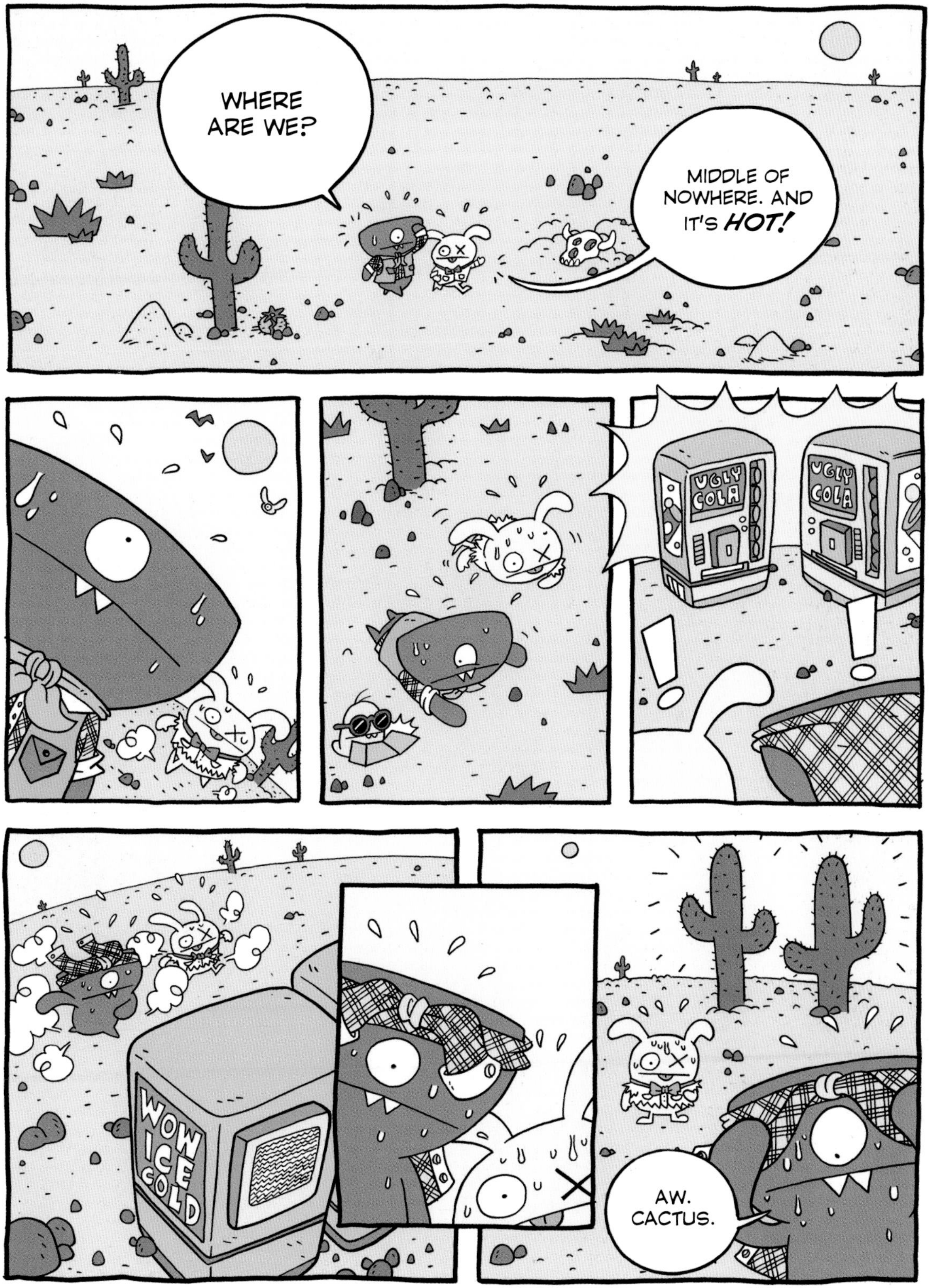
WHERE ARE WE?
MIDDLE OF NOWHERE. AND IT'S HOT!
UGLY COLA
UGLY COLA
WOW ICE COLD
AW. CACTUS.

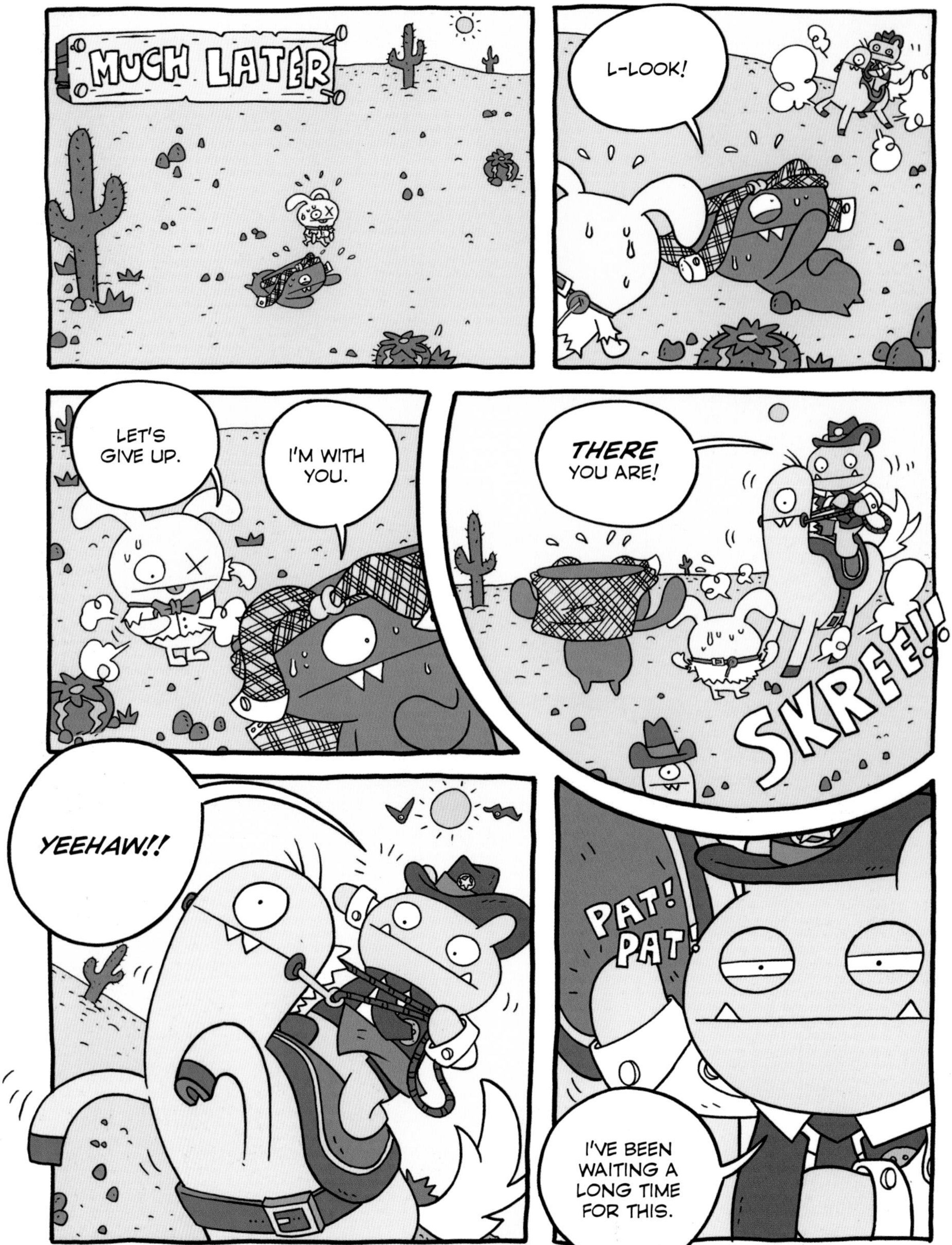
MUCH LATER
L-LOOK!
LET'S GIVE UP.
I'M WITH YOU.
THERE YOU ARE!
SKREE!!
YEEHAW!!
PAT! PAT!
I'VE BEEN WAITING A LONG TIME FOR THIS.

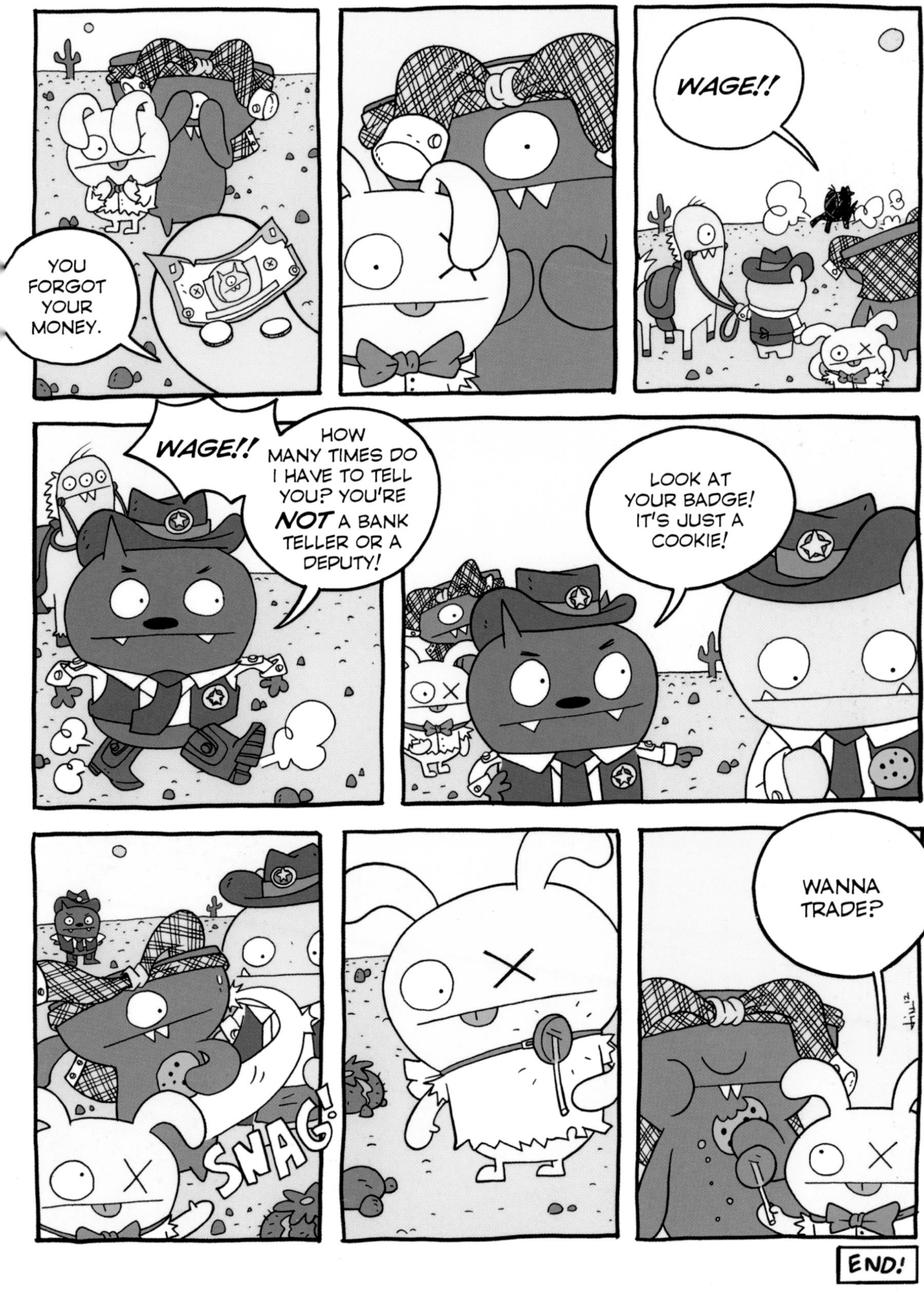
YOU FORGOT YOUR MONEY.
WAGE!!
WAGE!!
HOW MANY TIMES DO I HAVE TO TELL YOU? YOU'RE NOT A BANK TELLER OR A DEPUTY!
LOOK AT YOUR BADGE! IT'S JUST A COOKIE!
SNAG!
WANNA TRADE?
END!

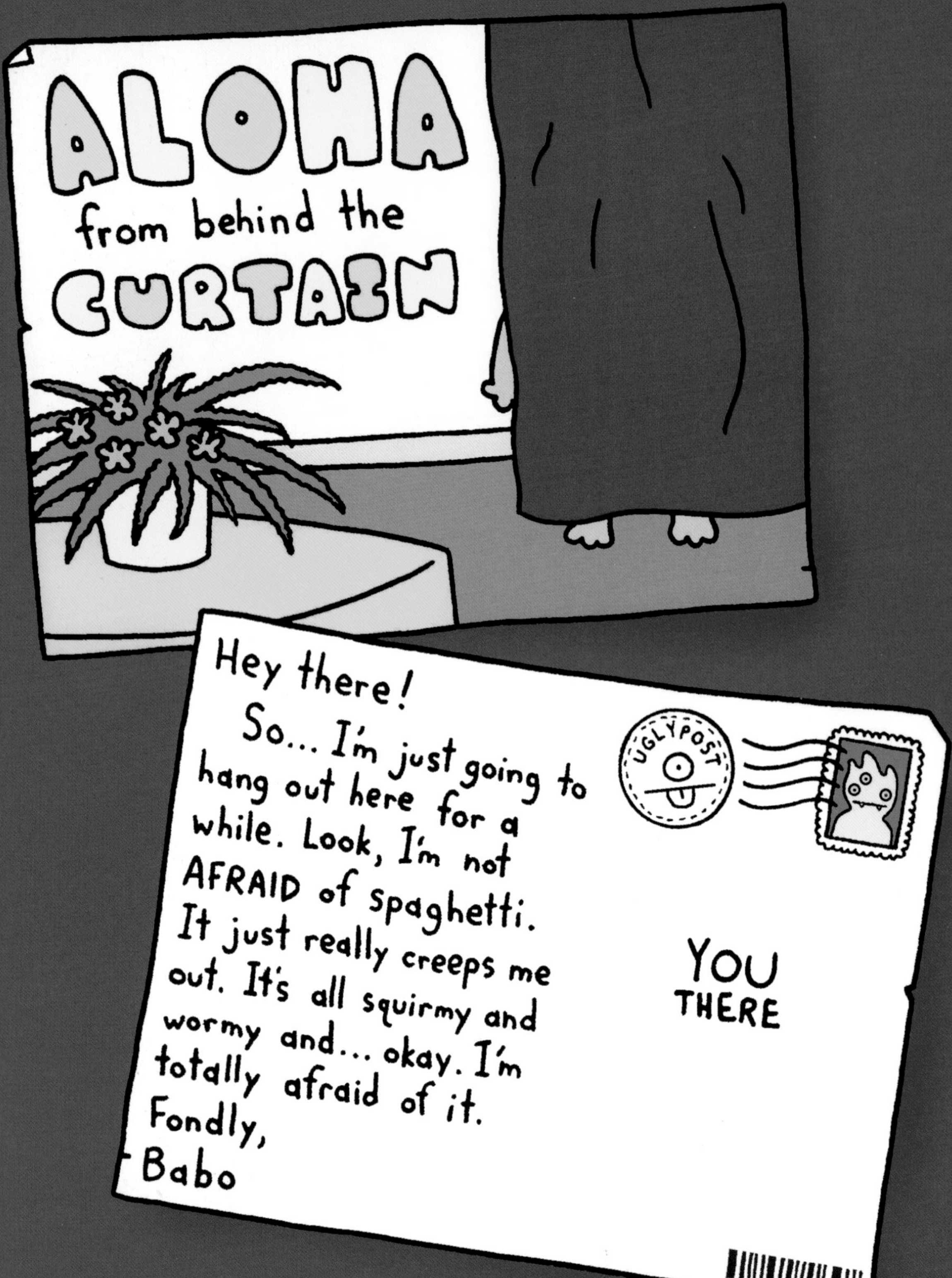
ALOHA
from behind the
CURTAIN
Hey there!
So... I'm just going to hang out here for a while. Look, I'm not AFRAID of spaghetti. It just really creeps me out. It's all squirmy and wormy and... okay. I'm totally afraid of it.
Fondly,
Babo
UGLYPOST
YOU
THERE

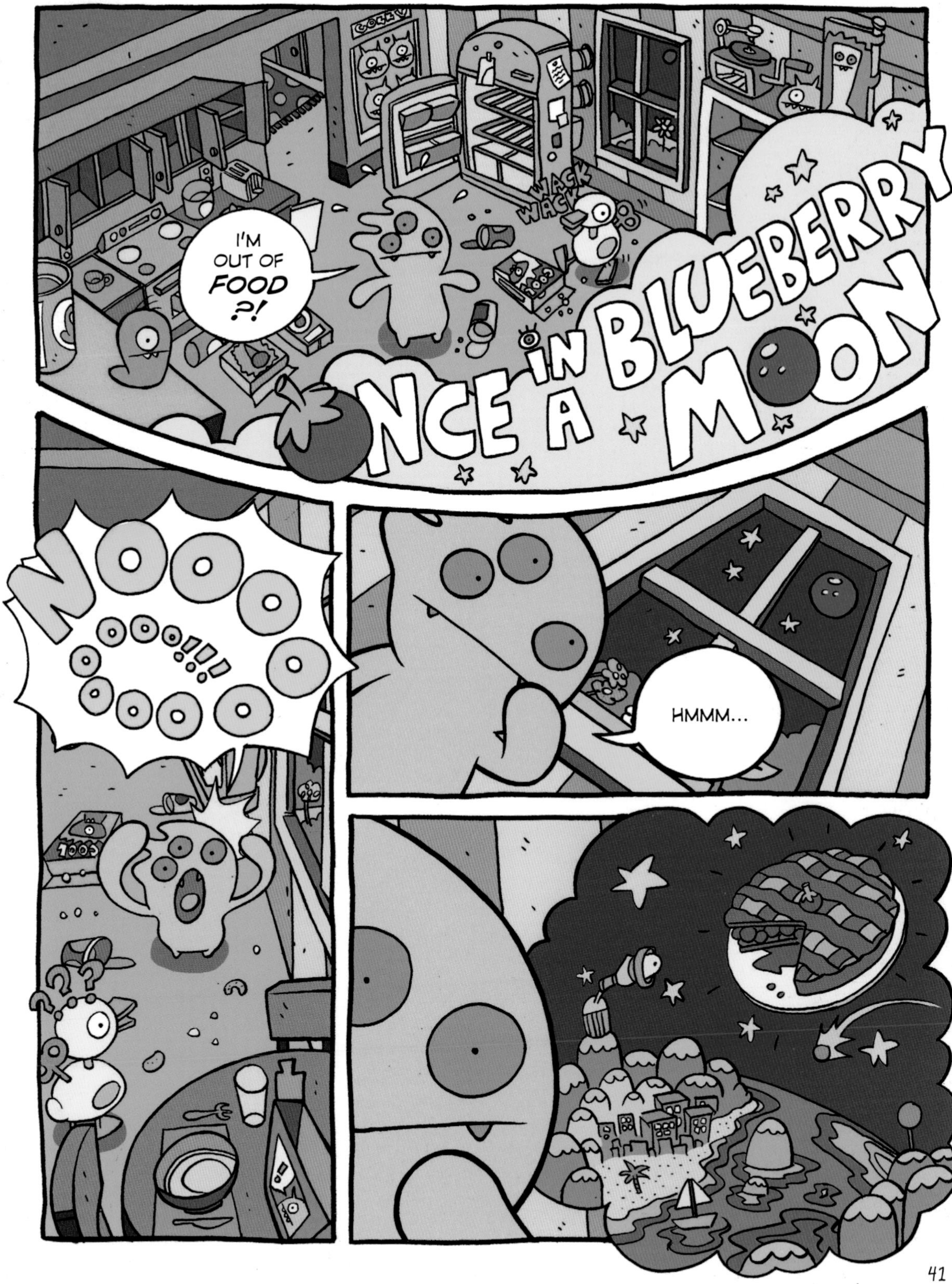

ONCE IN A BLUEBERRY MOON
I'M OUT OF FOOD ?!
WACK WACK
NOOOOOOOOOOOO!!!
HMMM...

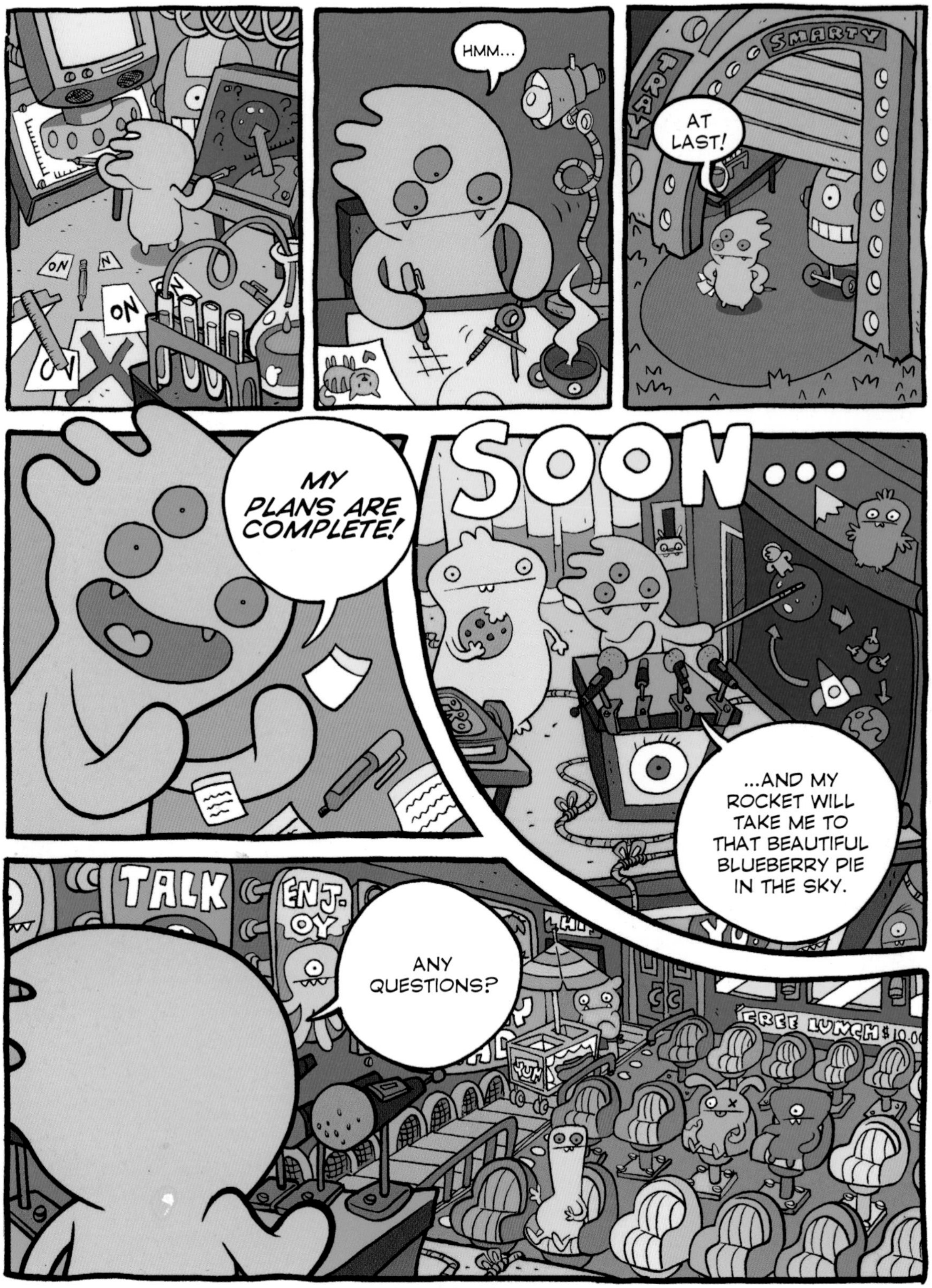
ON
N
ON
ON
HMM...
SMARTY
TRAY
AT LAST!
MY PLANS ARE COMPLETE!
SOON...
...AND MY ROCKET WILL TAKE ME TO THAT BEAUTIFUL BLUEBERRY PIE IN THE SKY.
TALK
ENJ-OY
ANY QUESTIONS?
FREE LUNCH

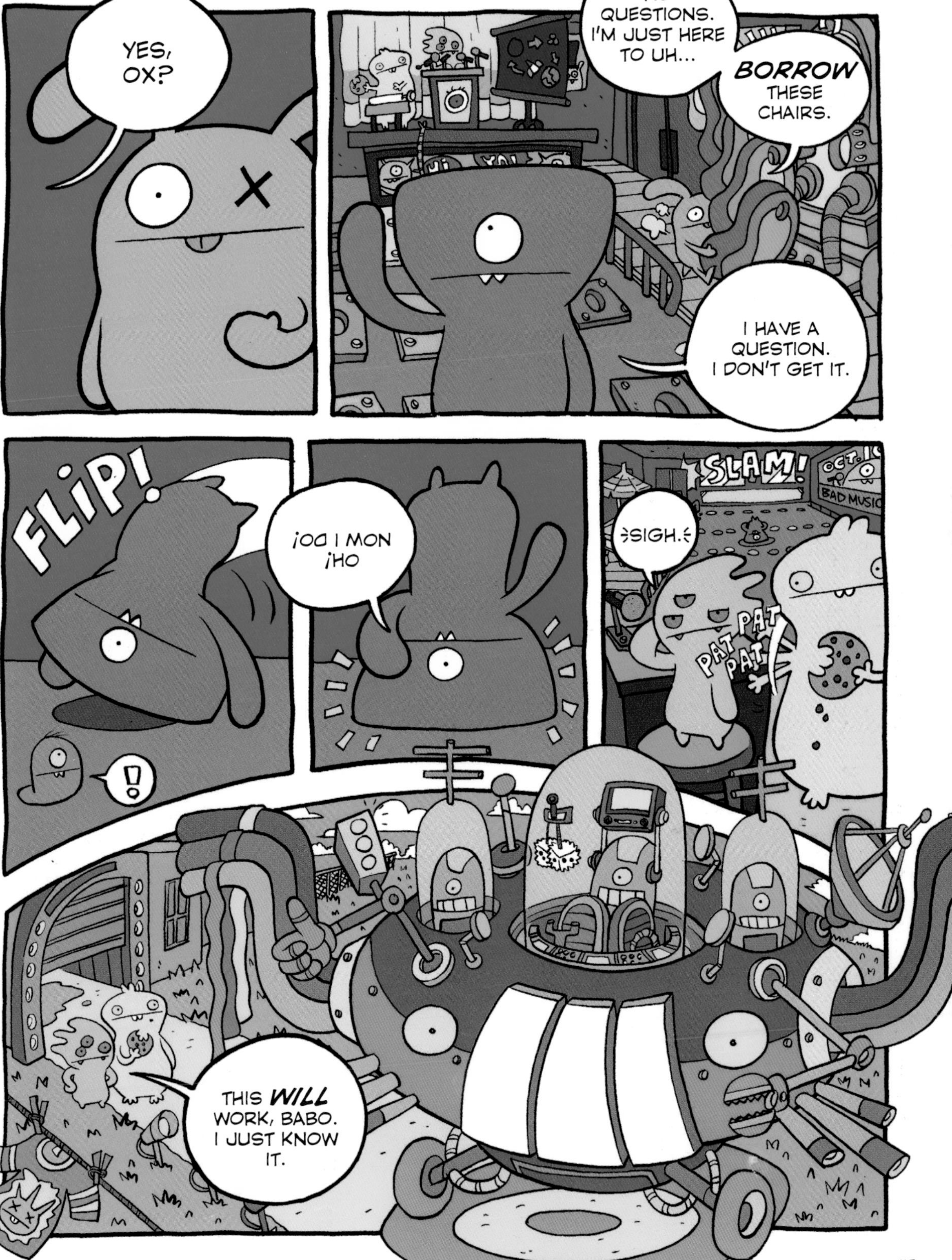
YES, OX?
NO QUESTIONS. I'M JUST HERE TO UH...
BORROW THESE CHAIRS.
I HAVE A QUESTION. I DON'T GET IT.
FLIP!
!
OH! NOW I DO!
SLAM!
BAD MUSIC
SIGH.
PAT PAT PAT PAT
THIS WILL WORK, BABO. I JUST KNOW IT.

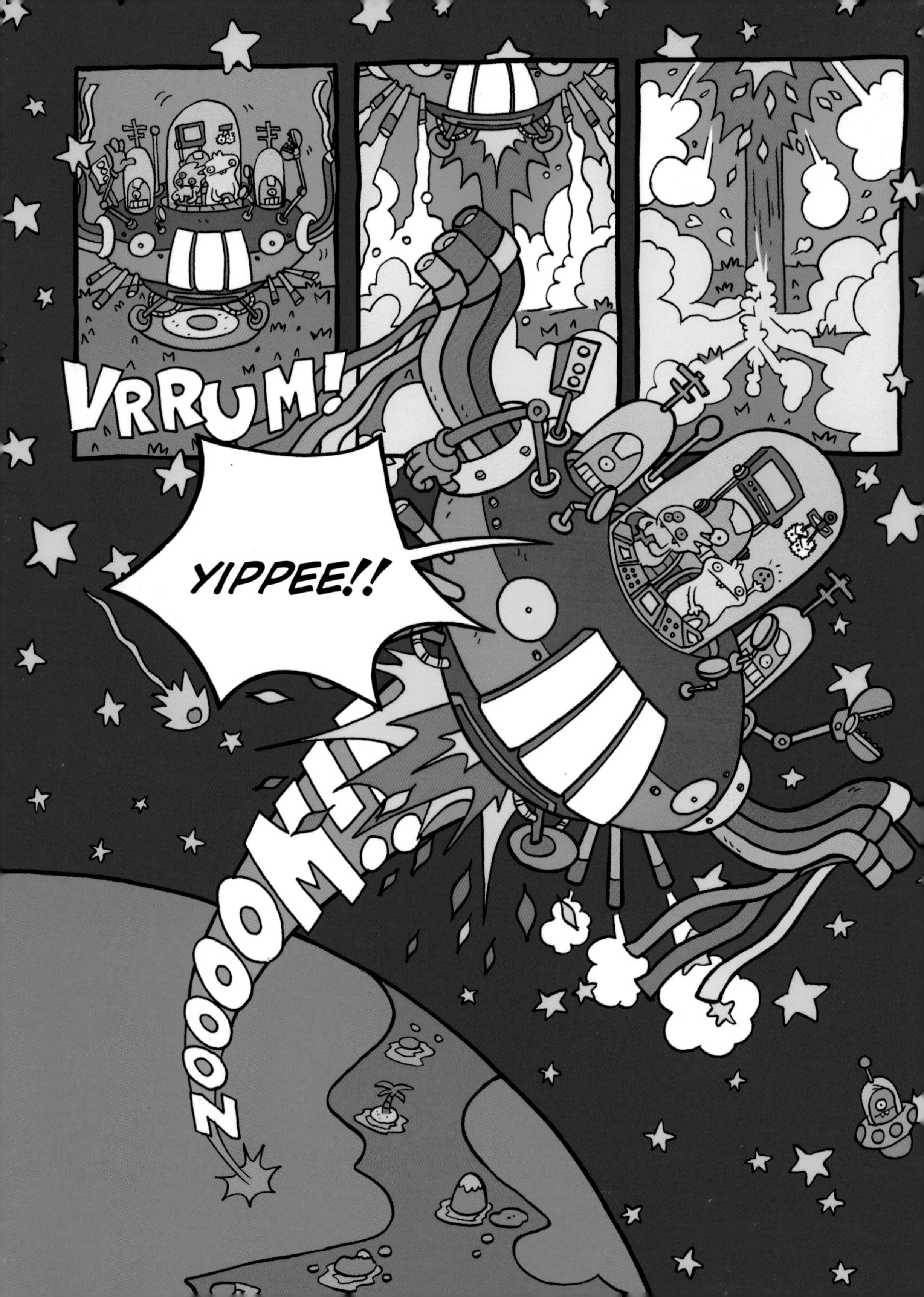

VRRUM!
YIPPEE!!
ZOOOOOOM...

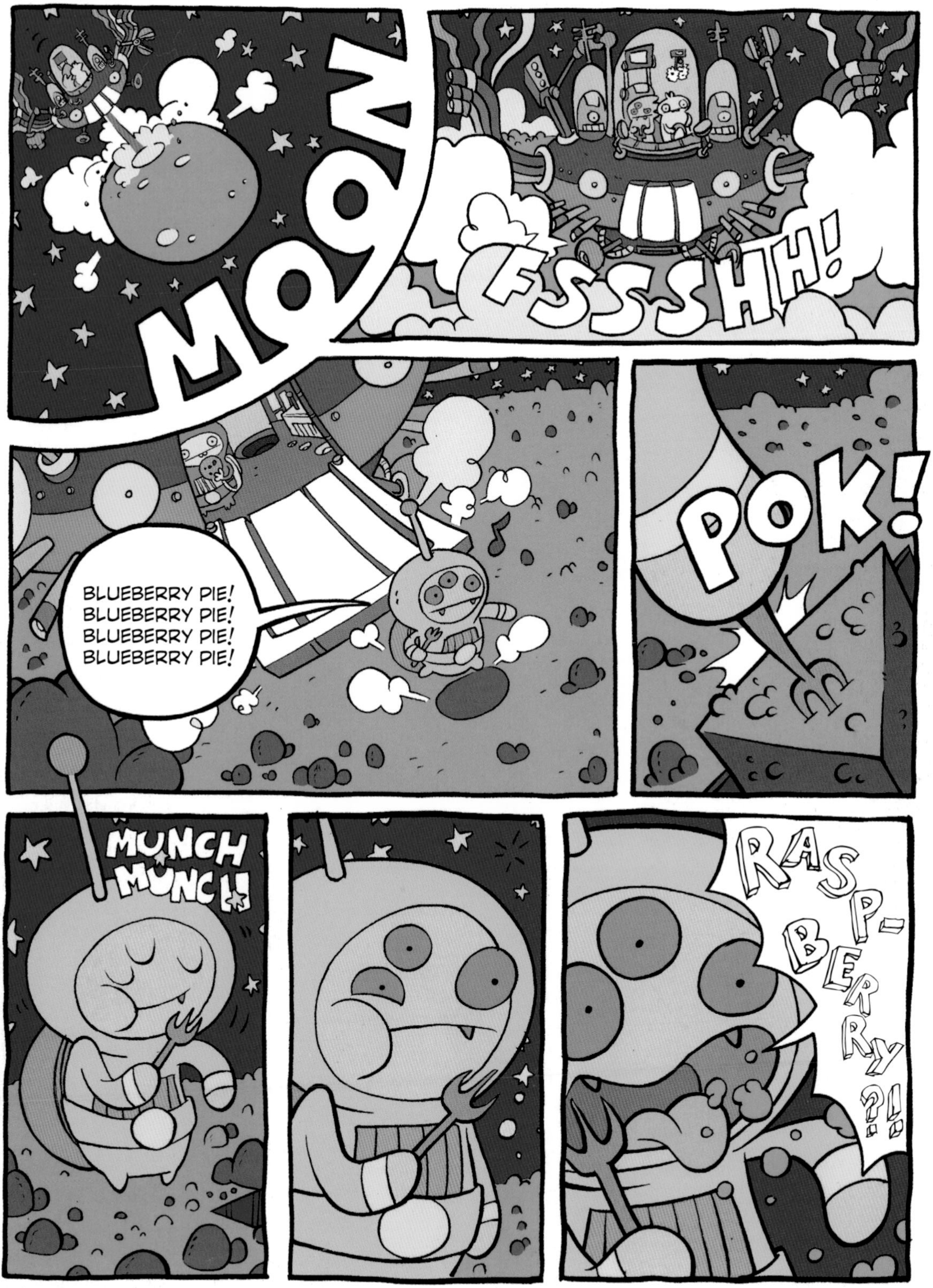
MOON
FSSSHH!
BLUEBERRY PIE! BLUEBERRY PIE! BLUEBERRY PIE! BLUEBERRY PIE!
POK!
MUNCH MUNCH
RASP-BERRY?!

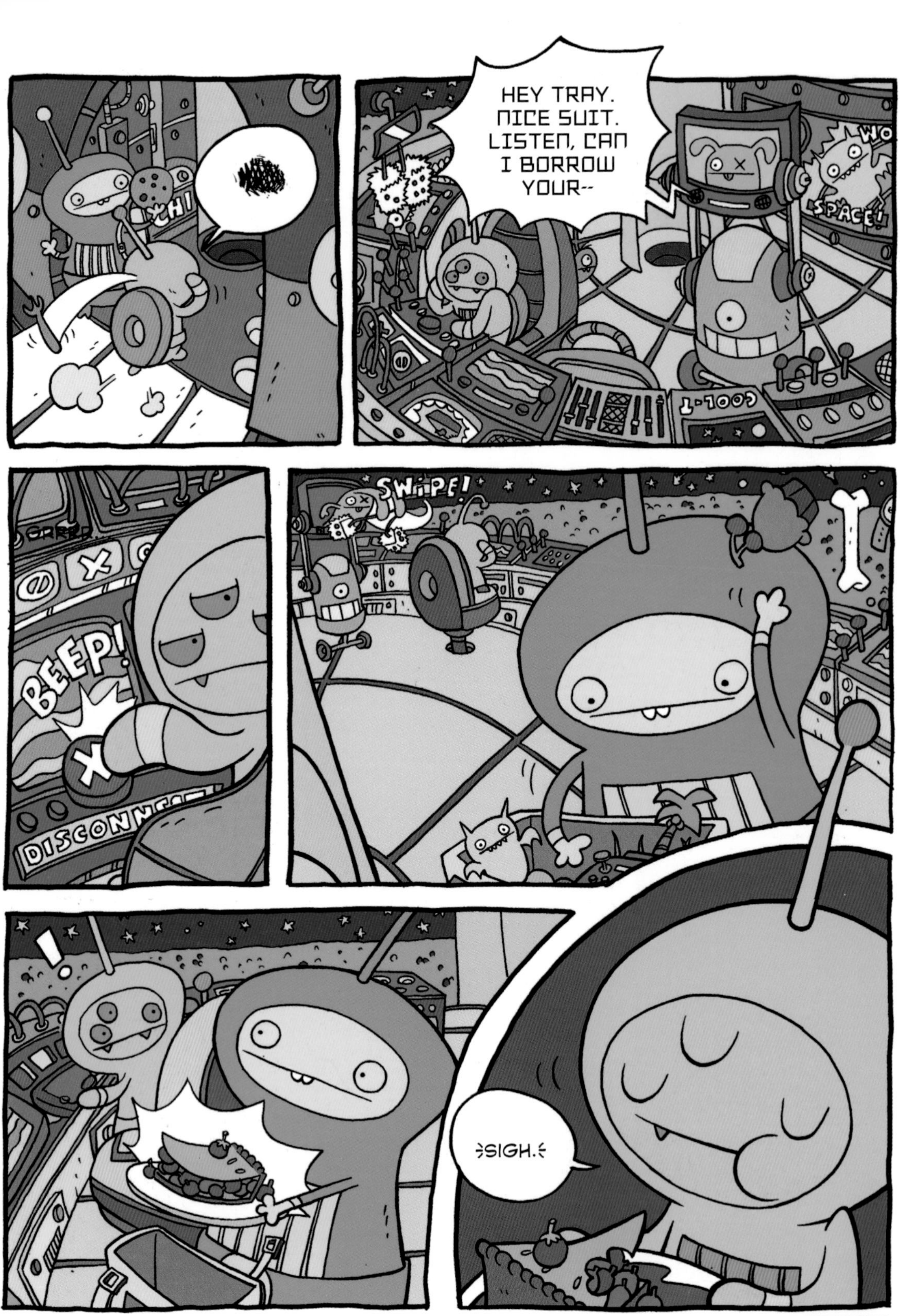
HEY TRAY. NICE SUIT. LISTEN, CAN I BORROW YOUR--
SPACE!
BEEP!
SWIPE!
!
SIGH.
END!

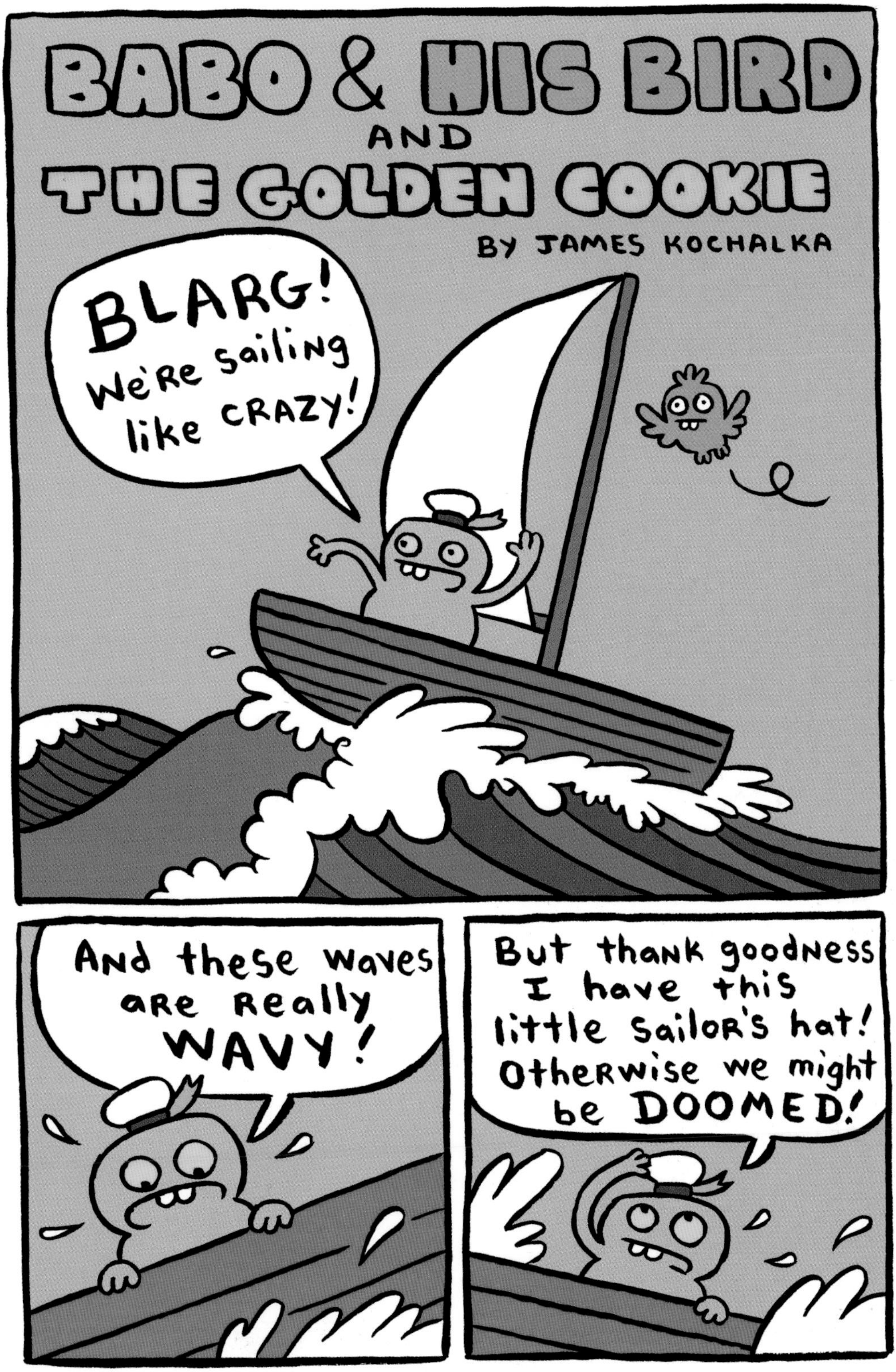
BABO & HIS BIRD
AND
THE GOLDEN COOKIE
BY JAMES KOCHALKA
BLARG! We're sailing like CRAZY!
And these waves are really WAVY!
But thank goodness I have this little sailor's hat! Otherwise we might be DOOMED!

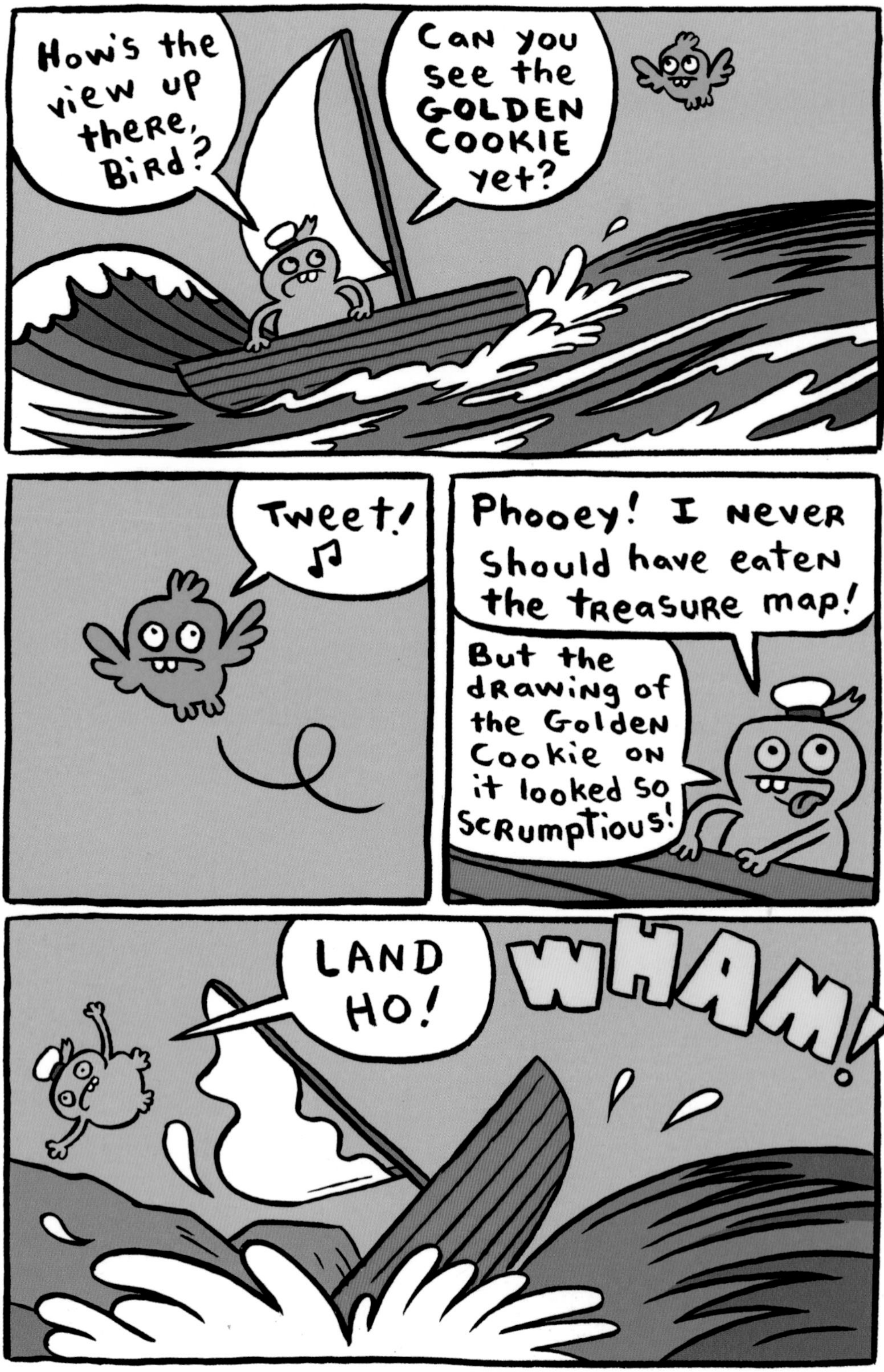
How's the view up there, Bird?
Can you see the GOLDEN COOKIE yet?
Tweet! ♫
Phooey! I never should have eaten the treasure map!
But the drawing of the Golden Cookie on it looked so scrumptious!
LAND HO!
WHAM!

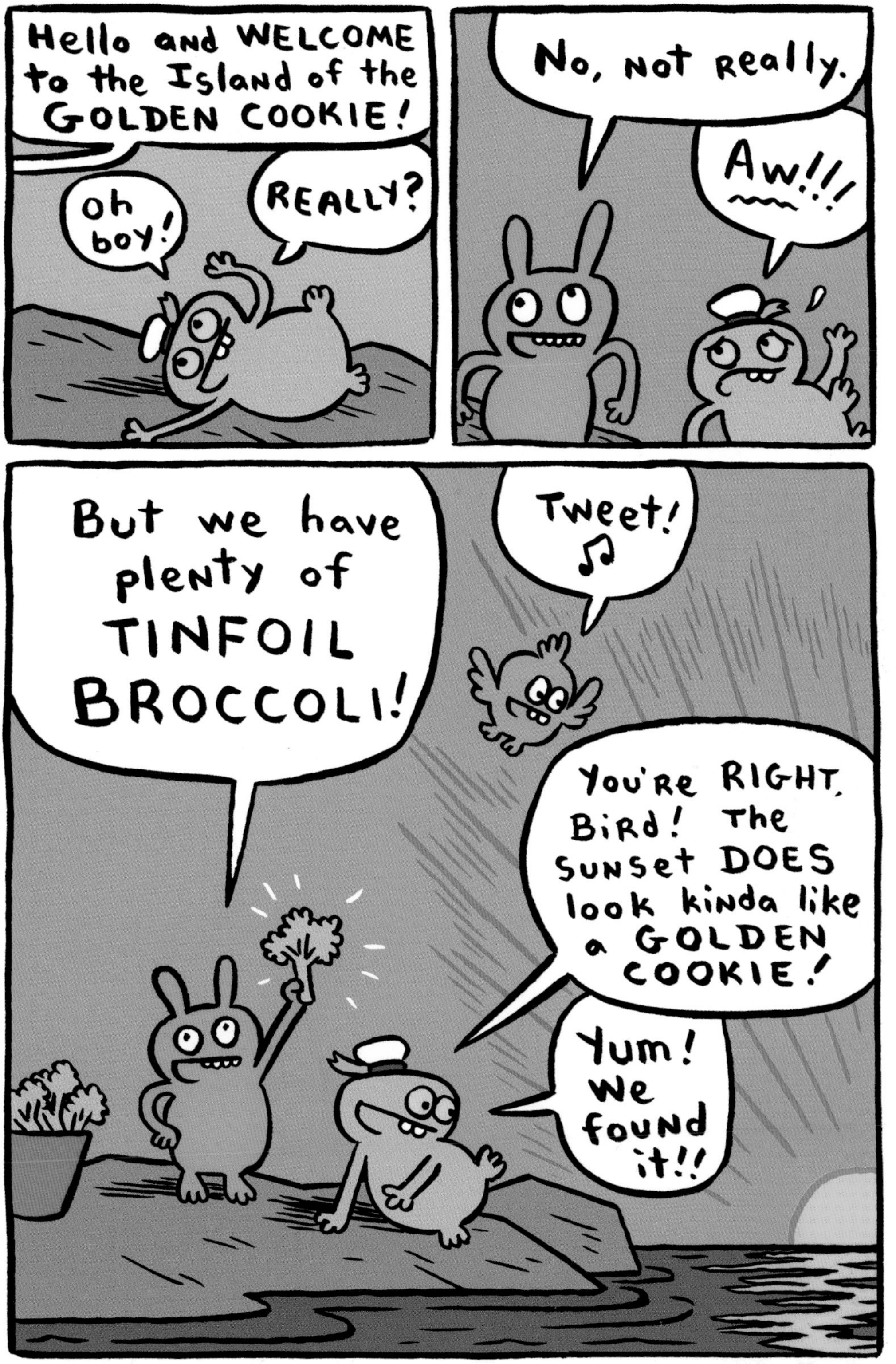
Hello and WELCOME to the Island of the GOLDEN COOKIE!
Oh boy!
REALLY?
No, not really.
Aw!!!
But we have plenty of TINFOIL BROCCOLI!
Tweet! ♫
You're RIGHT, Bird! The sunset DOES look kinda like a GOLDEN COOKIE!
Yum! We found it!!

THE END

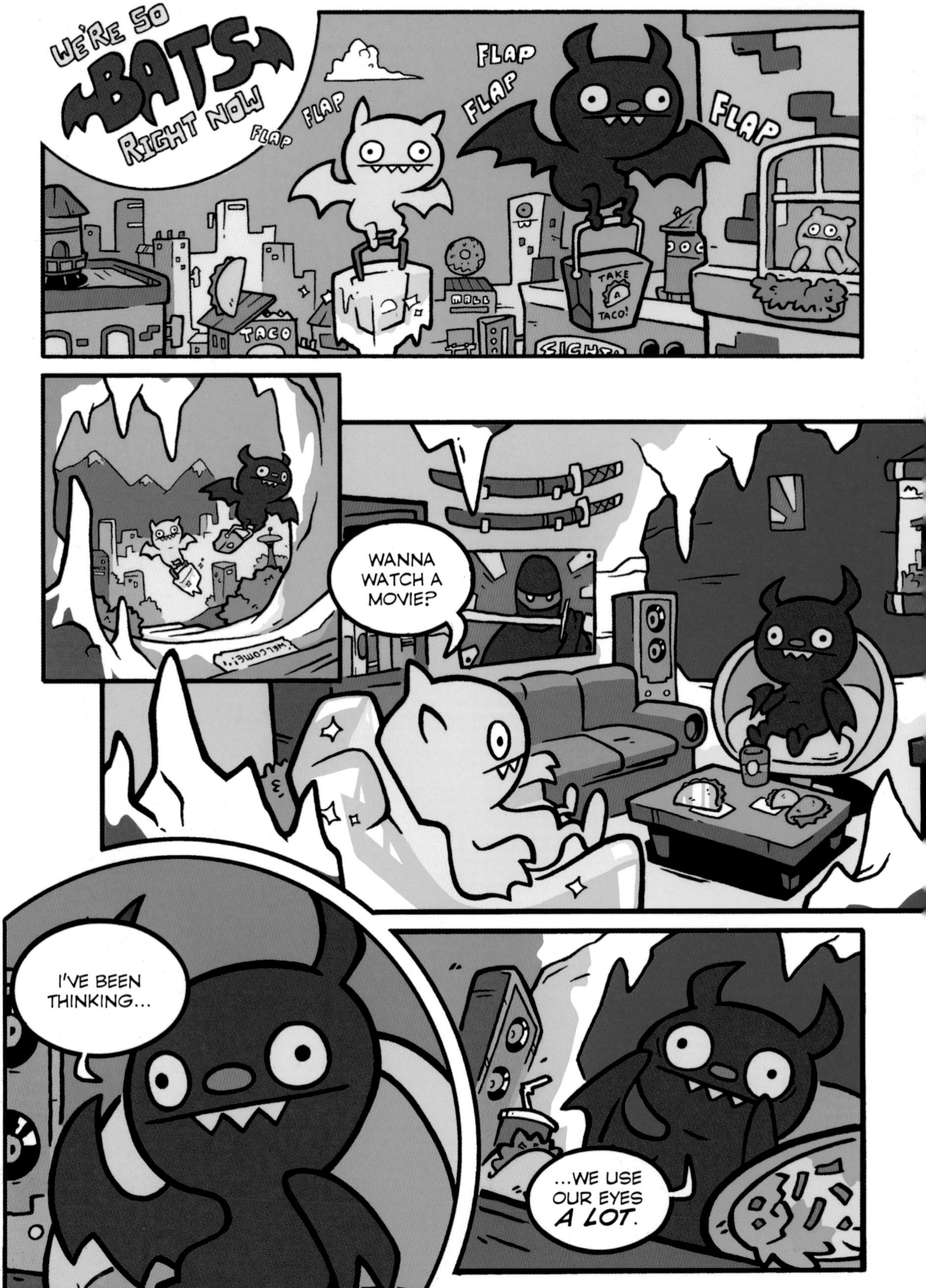
WE'RE SO BATS RIGHT NOW
FLAP FLAP
FLAP FLAP
FLAP FLAP
TACO
MALL
TAKE A TACO!
WELCOME!
WANNA WATCH A MOVIE?
I'VE BEEN THINKING...
...WE USE OUR EYES A LOT.

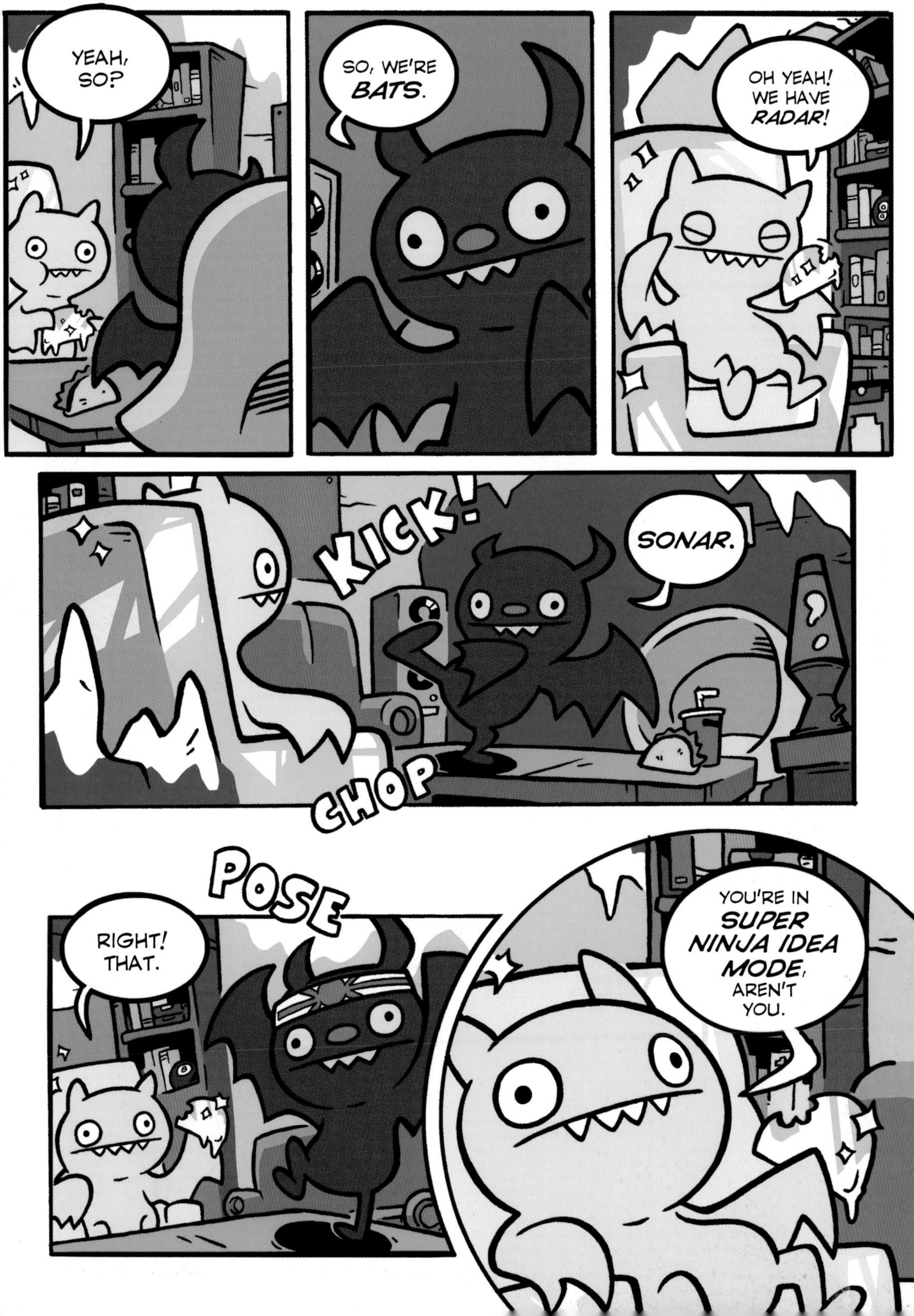

YEAH, SO?
SO, WE'RE BATS.
OH YEAH! WE HAVE RADAR!
KICK!
SONAR.
CHOP
POSE
RIGHT! THAT.
YOU'RE IN SUPER NINJA IDEA MODE, AREN'T YOU.

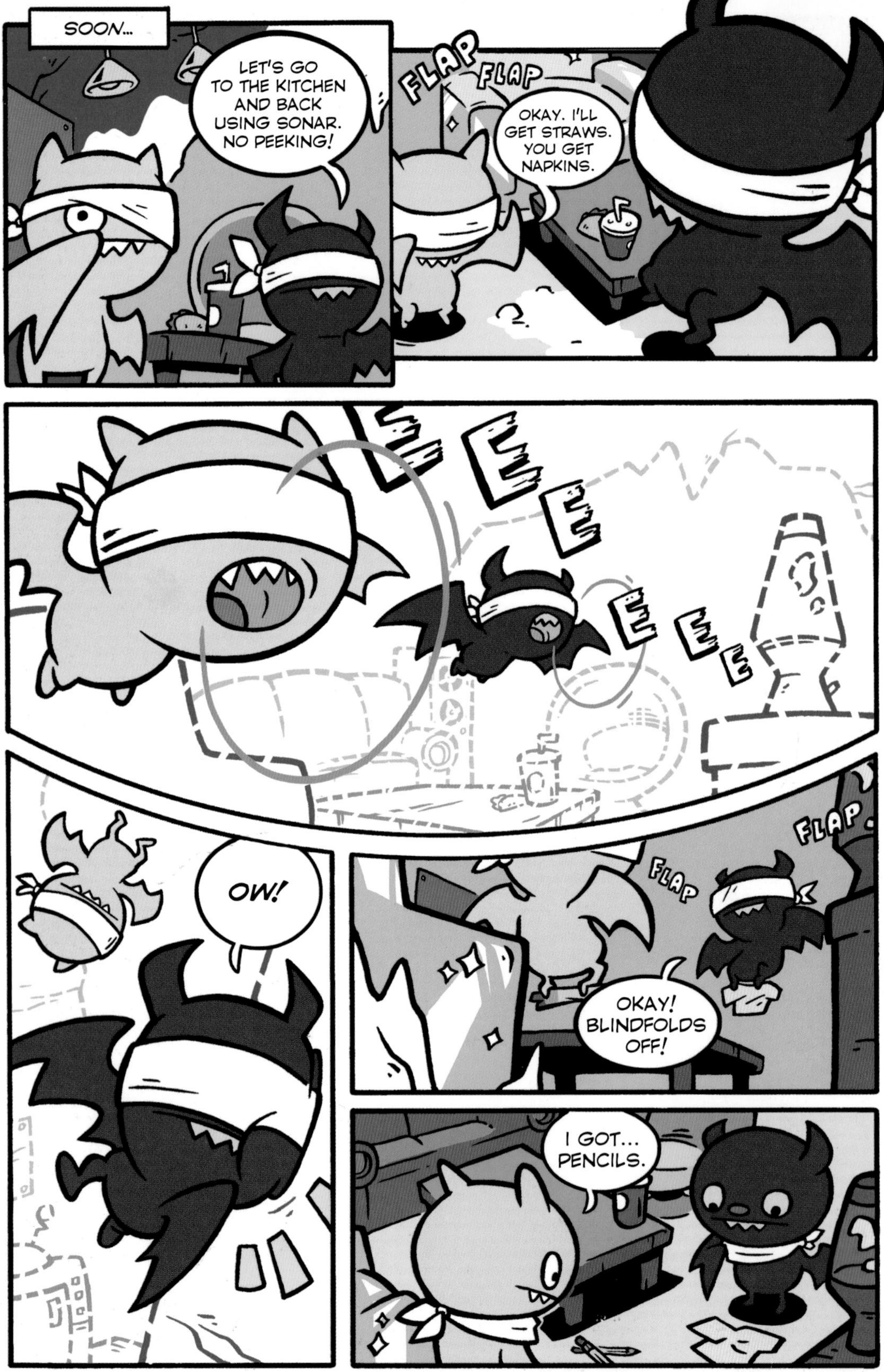
SOON...
LET'S GO TO THE KITCHEN AND BACK USING SONAR. NO PEEKING!
FLAP FLAP
OKAY. I'LL GET STRAWS. YOU GET NAPKINS.
EEEEEEEEE
OW!
FLAP FLAP
OKAY! BLINDFOLDS OFF!
I GOT... PENCILS.

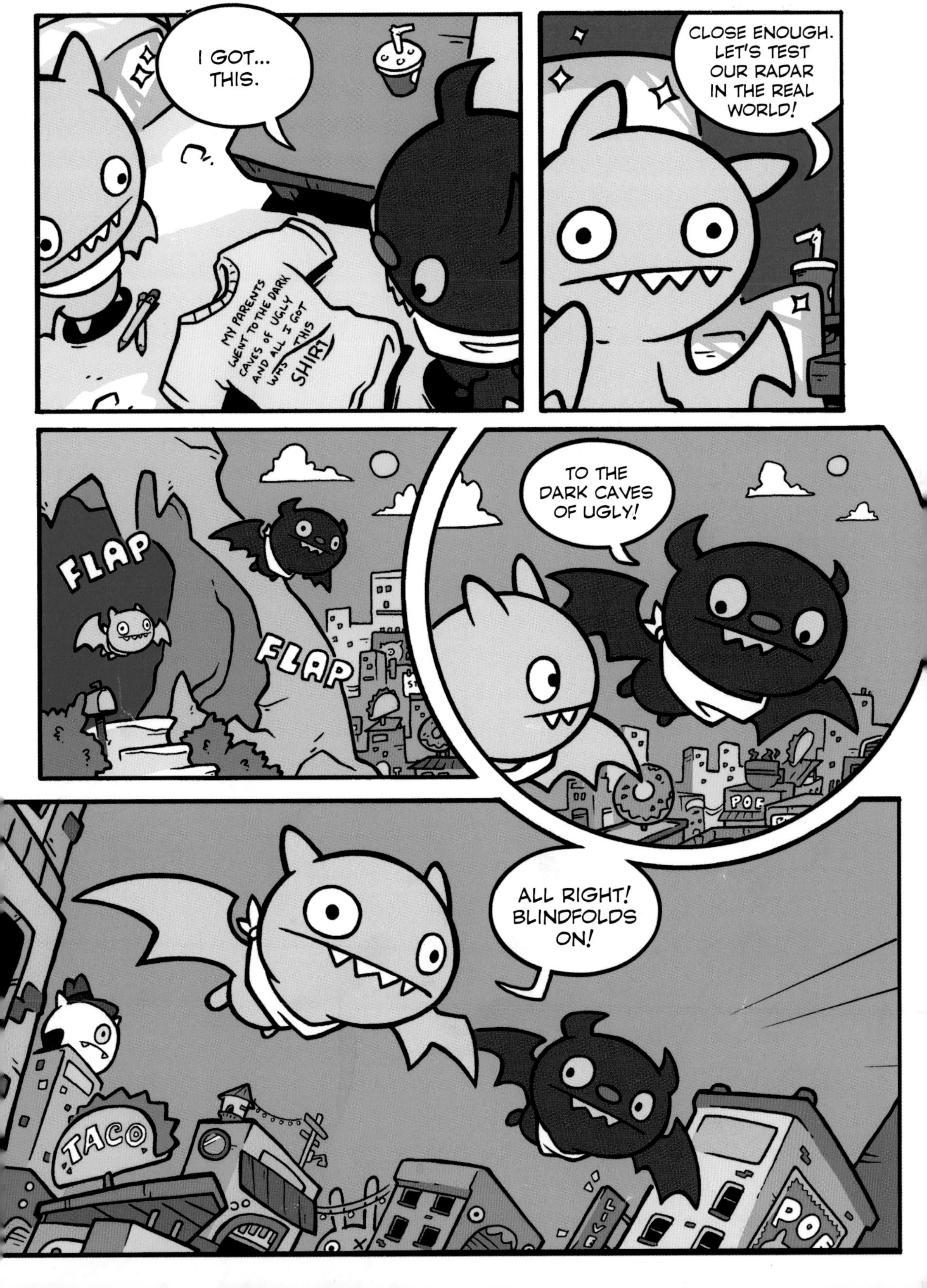
I GOT... THIS.
MY PARENTS WENT TO THE DARK CAVES OF UGLY AND ALL I GOT WAS THIS SHIRT
CLOSE ENOUGH. LET'S TEST OUR RADAR IN THE REAL WORLD!
FLAP
FLAP
TO THE DARK CAVES OF UGLY!
POE
ALL RIGHT! BLINDFOLDS ON!
TACO
POE

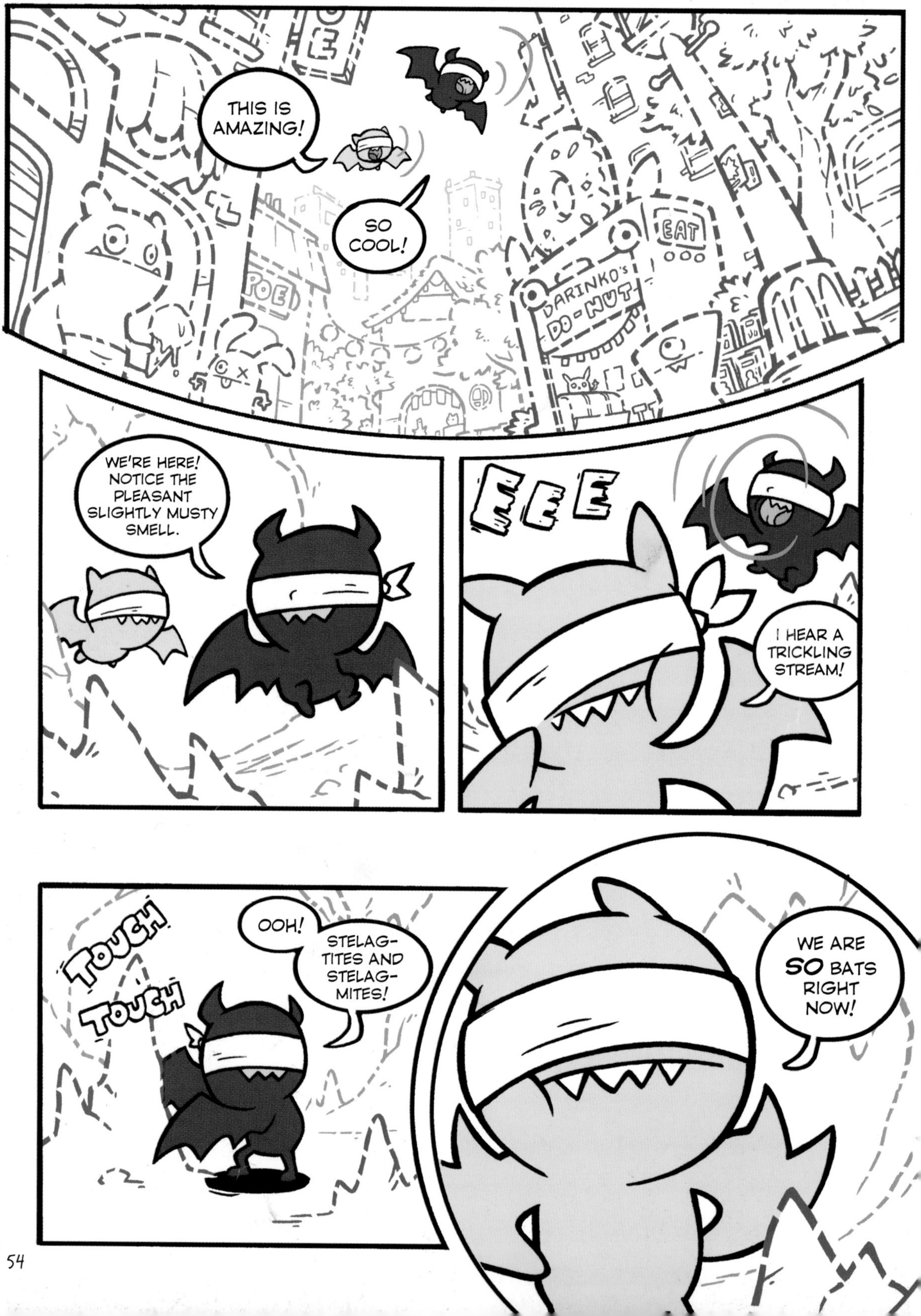
THIS IS AMAZING!
SO COOL!
EAT
DARINKO'S DO-NUT
WE'RE HERE! NOTICE THE PLEASANT SLIGHTLY MUSTY SMELL.
EEE
I HEAR A TRICKLING STREAM!
TOUCH
TOUCH
OOH!
STELAG-TITES AND STELAG-MITES!
WE ARE SO BATS RIGHT NOW!

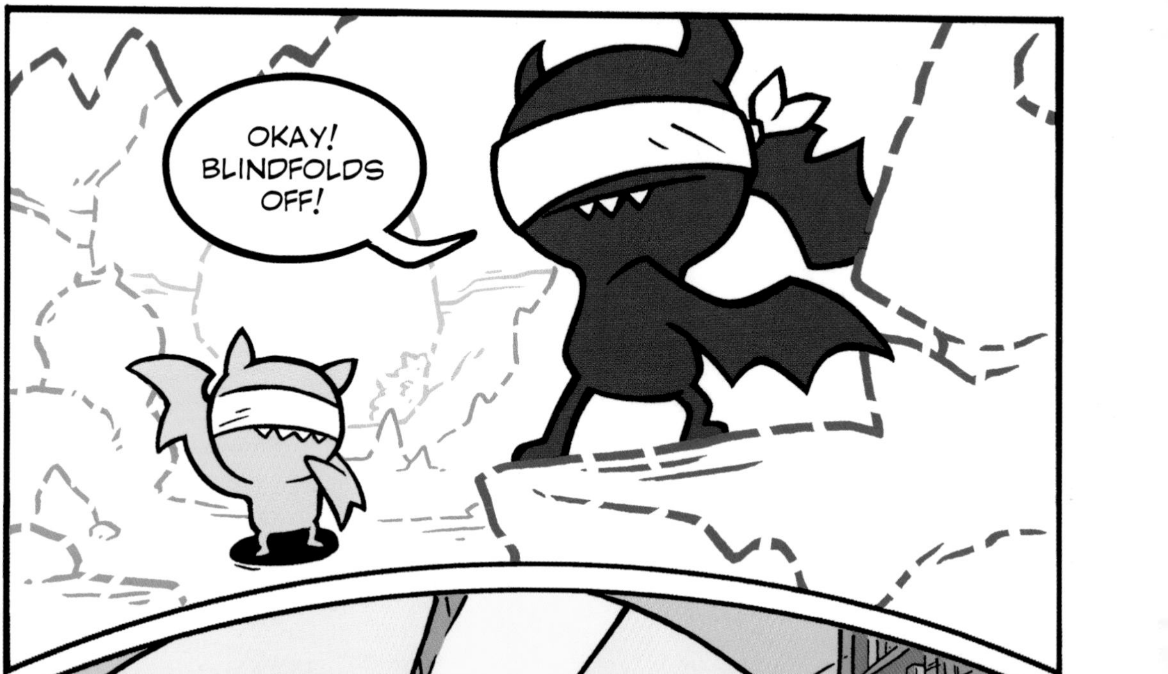
OKAY! BLINDFOLDS OFF!

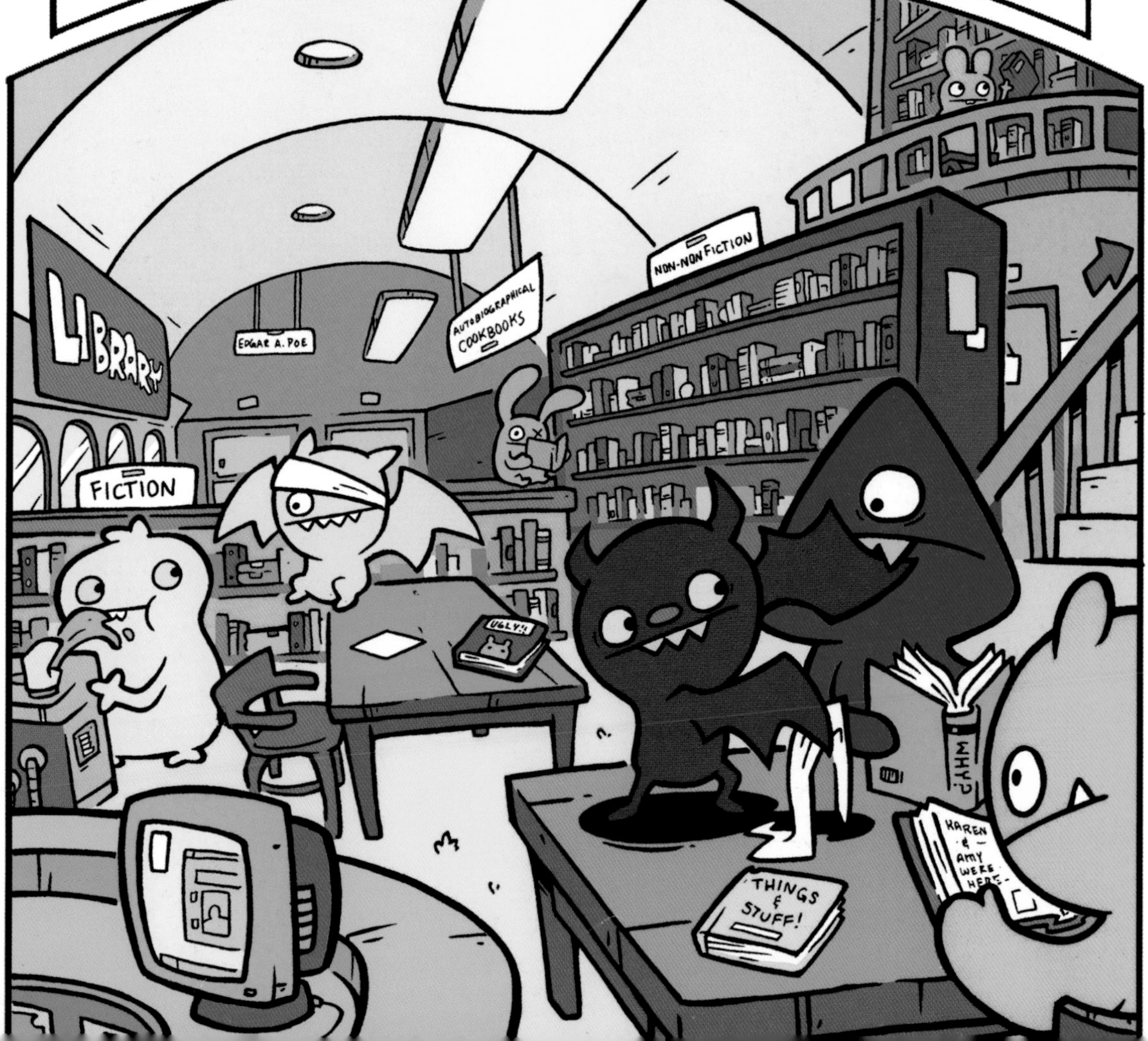
LIBRARY
EDGAR A. POE
AUTOBIOGRAPHICAL COOKBOOKS
NON-NONFICTION
FICTION
UGLY!
WHY?
THINGS & STUFF!
KAREN & AMY WERE HERE

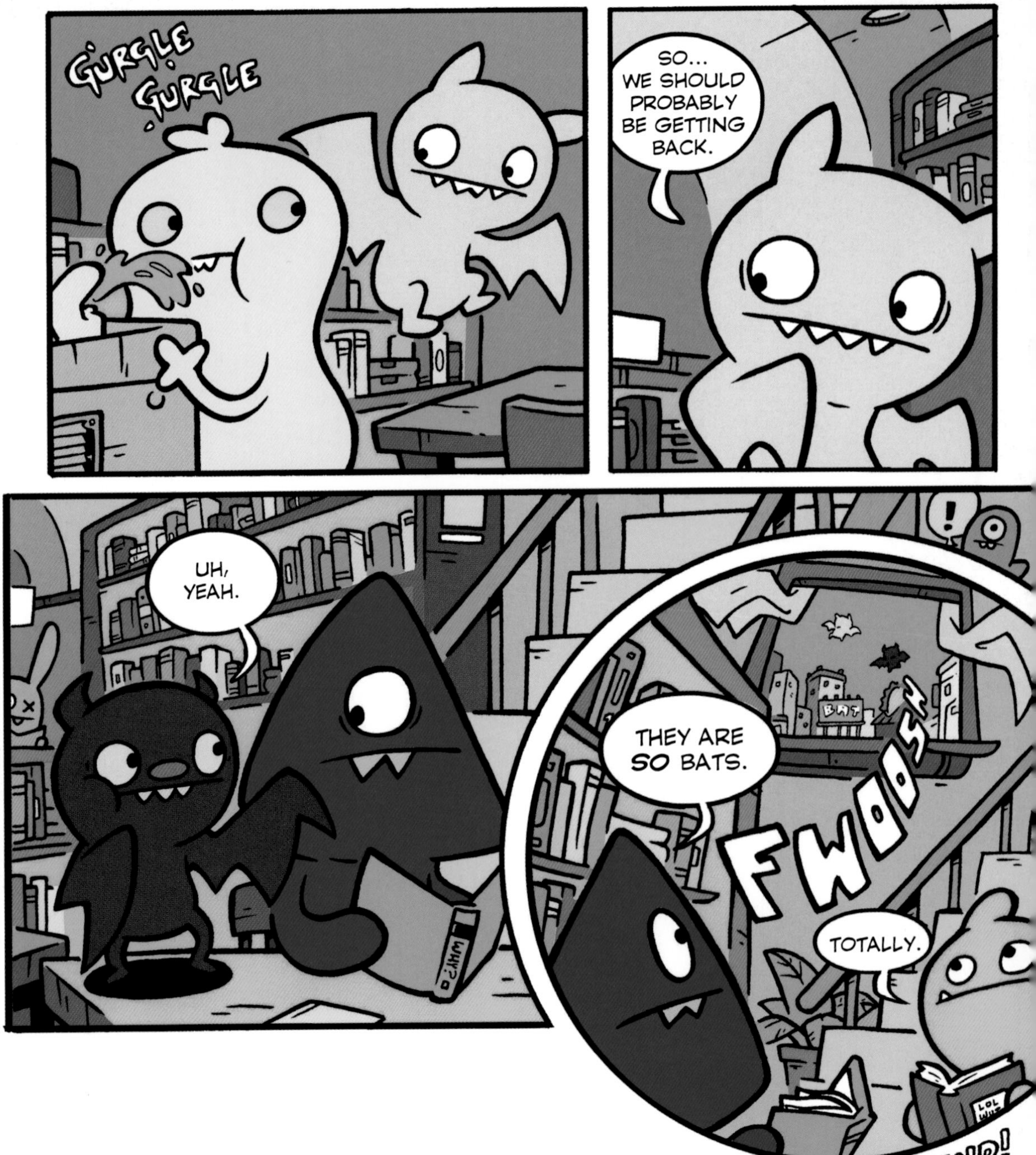
GURGLE GURGLE
SO... WE SHOULD PROBABLY BE GETTING BACK.
UH, YEAH.
!
THEY ARE SO BATS.
BAT
FWOOSH
TOTALLY.
END!

FROZEN PRETZELS

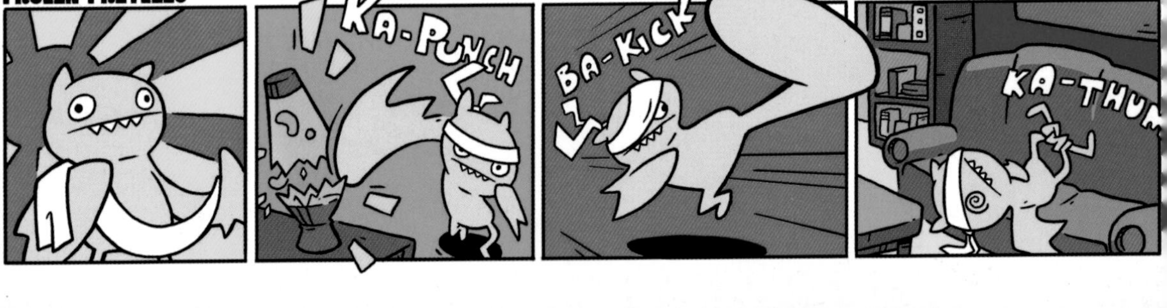
KA-PUNCH
BA-KICK
KA-THU

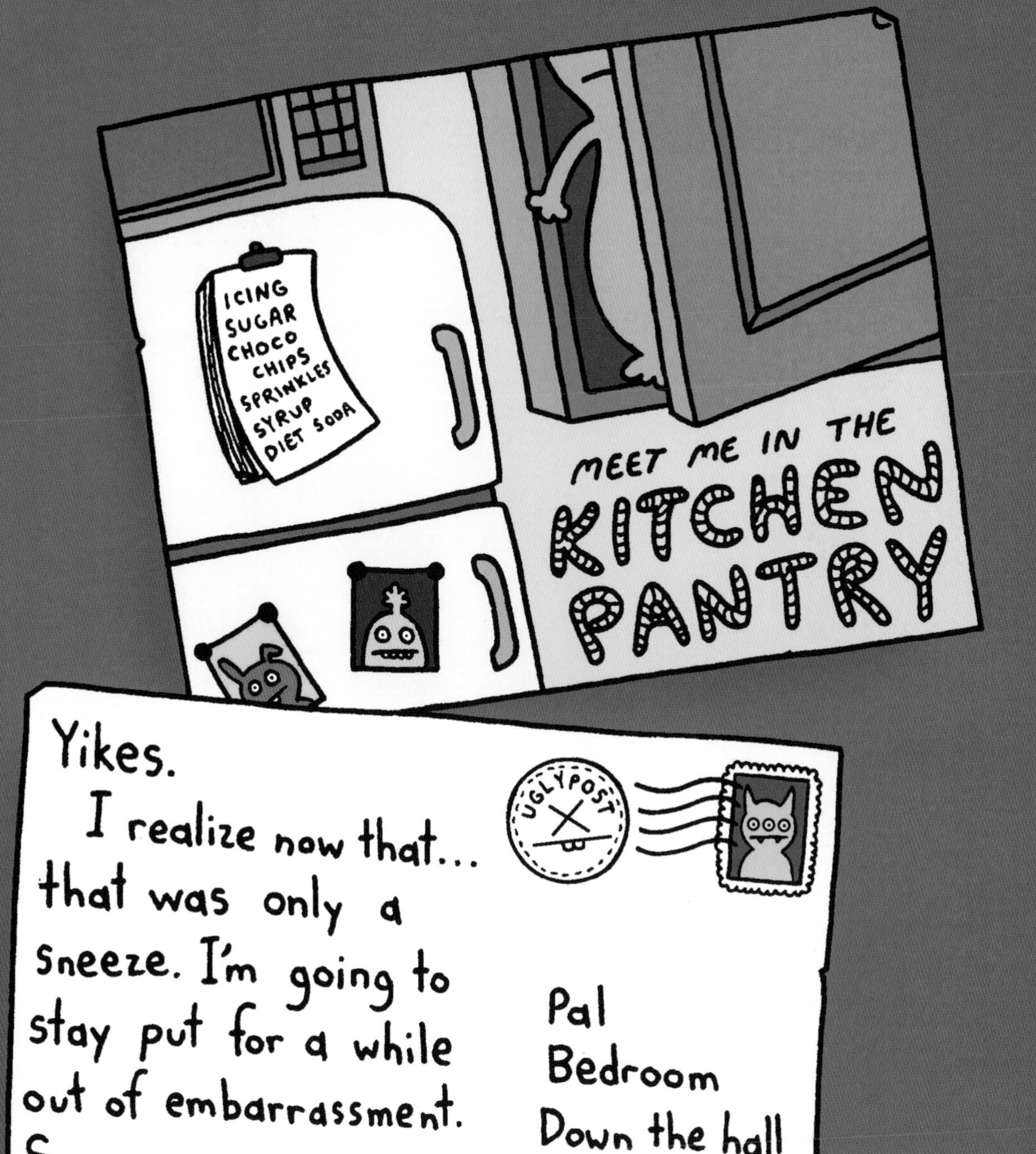
ICING
SUGAR
CHOCO
CHIPS
SPRINKLES
SYRUP
DIET SODA
MEET ME IN THE
KITCHEN
PANTRY
Yikes.
I realize now that...
that was only a
sneeze. I'm going to
stay put for a while
out of embarrassment.
Sorry,
Babo
P.S. Guh-zooondhite!
UGLYPOST
Pal
Bedroom
Down the hall

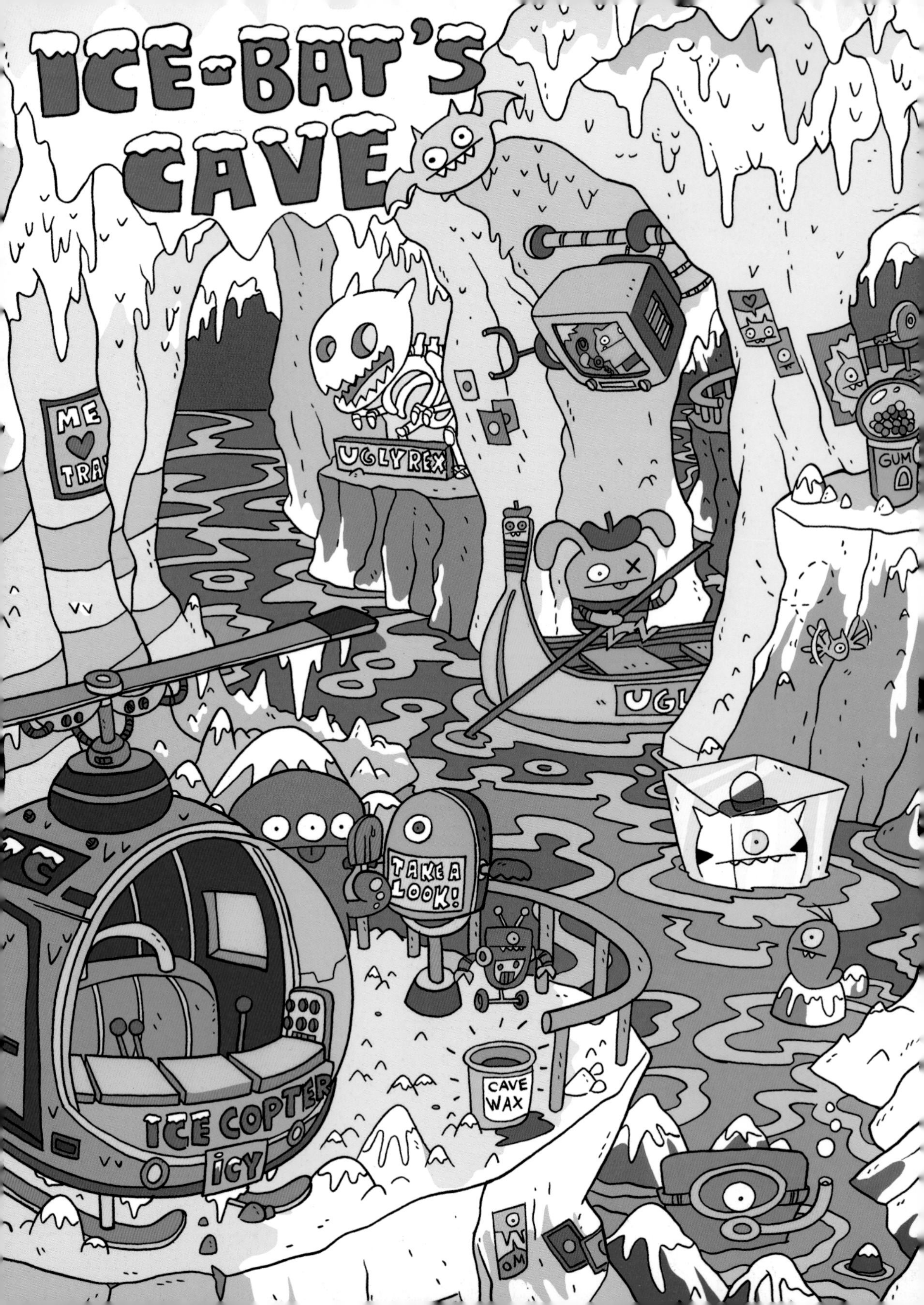
ICE-BAT'S CAVE
ME ♥ TRA
UGLYREX
GUM
UGL
TAKE A LOOK!
CAVE WAX
ICE COPTER
ICY

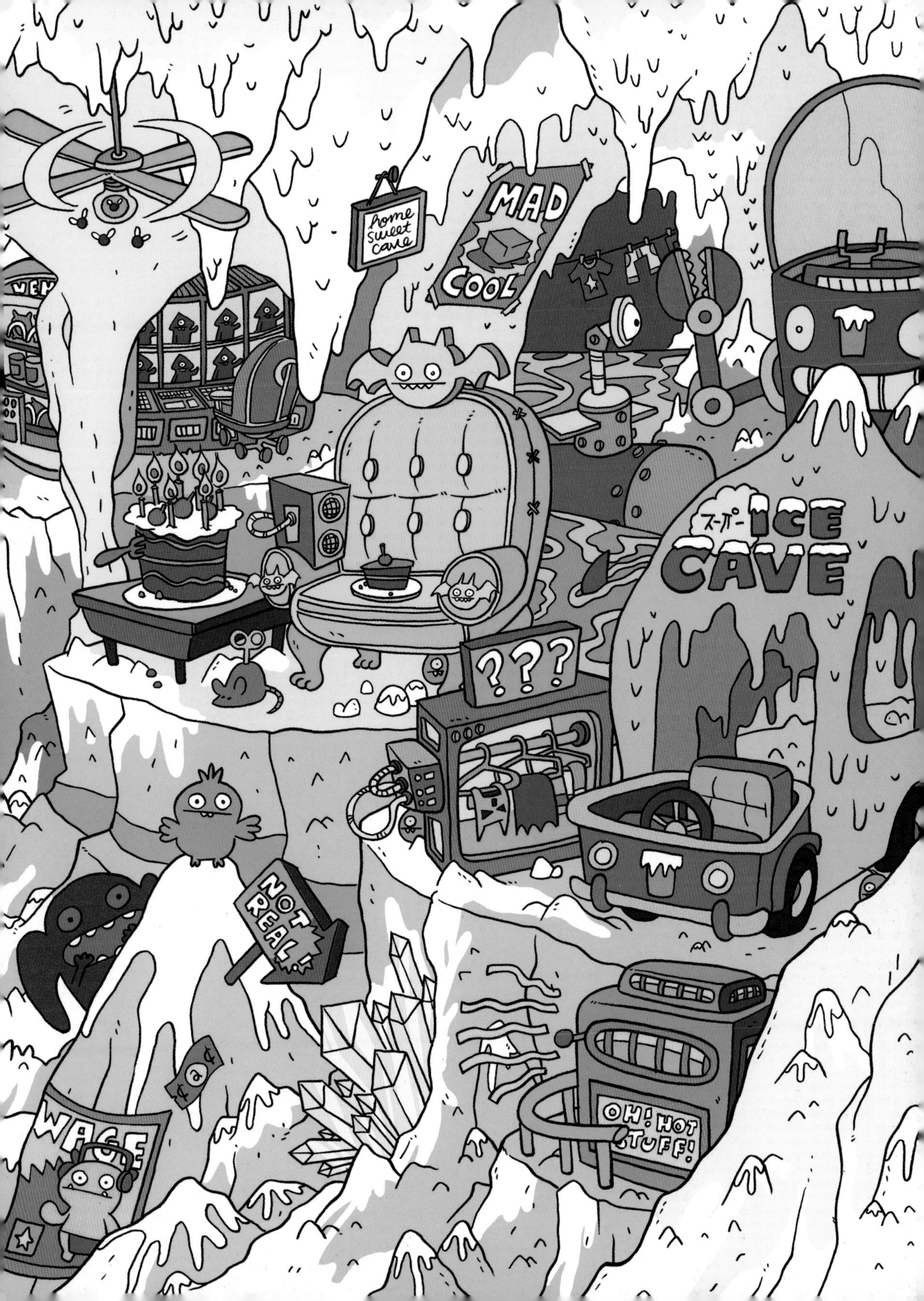
home sweet cave
MAD
COOL
スーパー ICE CAVE
???
NOT REAL!
WAGE
OH! HOT STUFF!

AHOY, ME UGLYS!

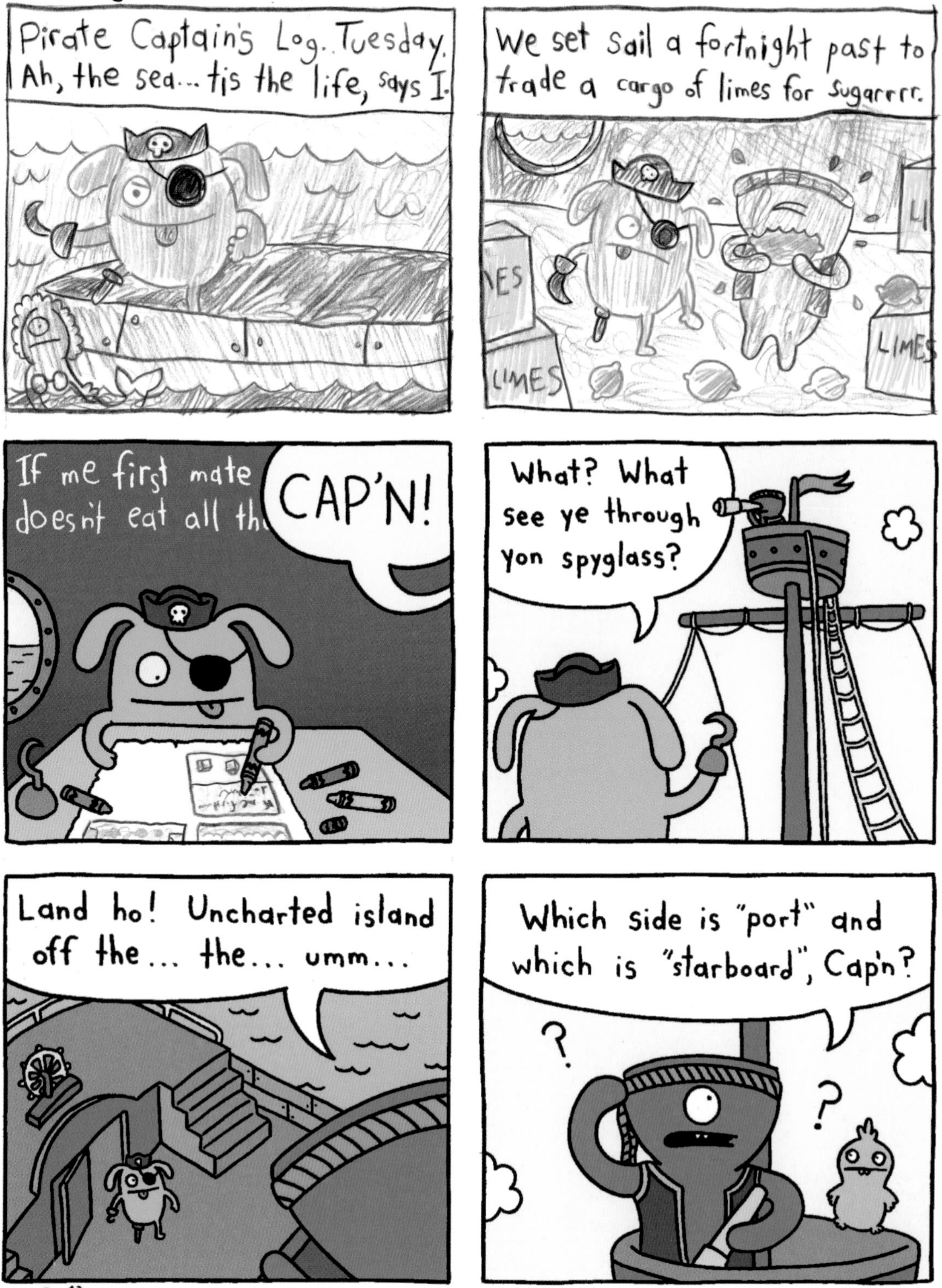

Pirate Captain's Log.. Tuesday. Ah, the sea... tis the life, says I.
We set sail a fortnight past to trade a cargo of limes for sugarrrr.
LIMES
LIMES
LIMES
If me first mate doesn't eat all th
CAP'N!
What? What see ye through yon spyglass?
Land ho! Uncharted island off the... the... umm...
Which side is "port" and which is "starboard", Cap'n?
?
?

TRAVIS NICHOLS

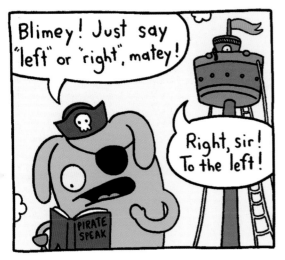

Blimey! Just say "left" or "right", matey!

Right, sir! To the left!

PIRATE SPEAK

Make ready the tender! Could be a great place to bury some treasure, says I!

Aye, sir! And I could go for some fresh coconut water.

You really can't beat fresh coconut water.

Especially with a—

AVAST! Who goes there?!

RRRRAAAUUGGGHHH!!!

Whoa. Whoa. Friend.

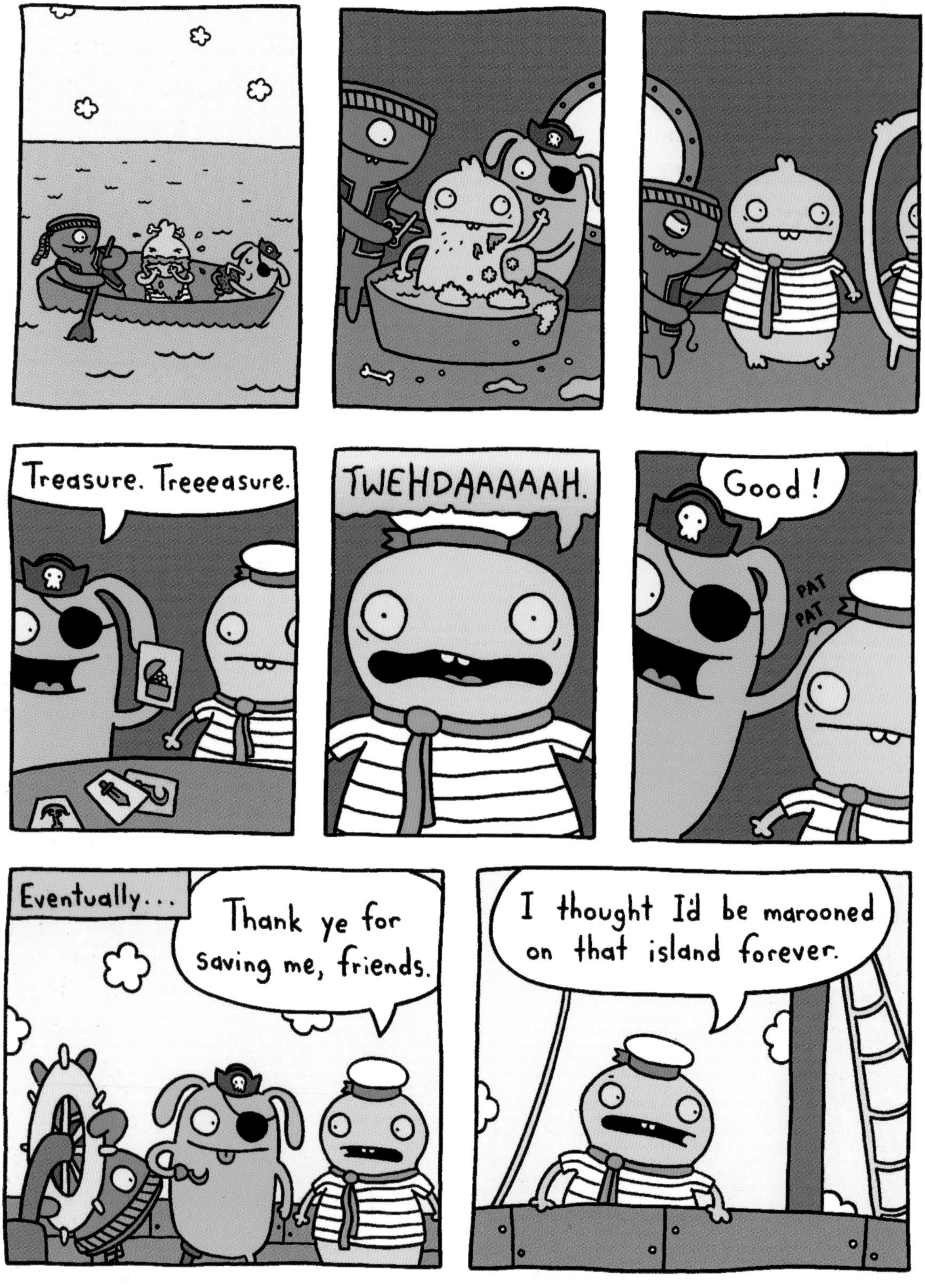
Treasure. Treeeasure.
TWEHDAAAAAH.
Good!
PAT PAT
Eventually...
Thank ye for saving me, friends.
I thought I'd be marooned on that island forever.

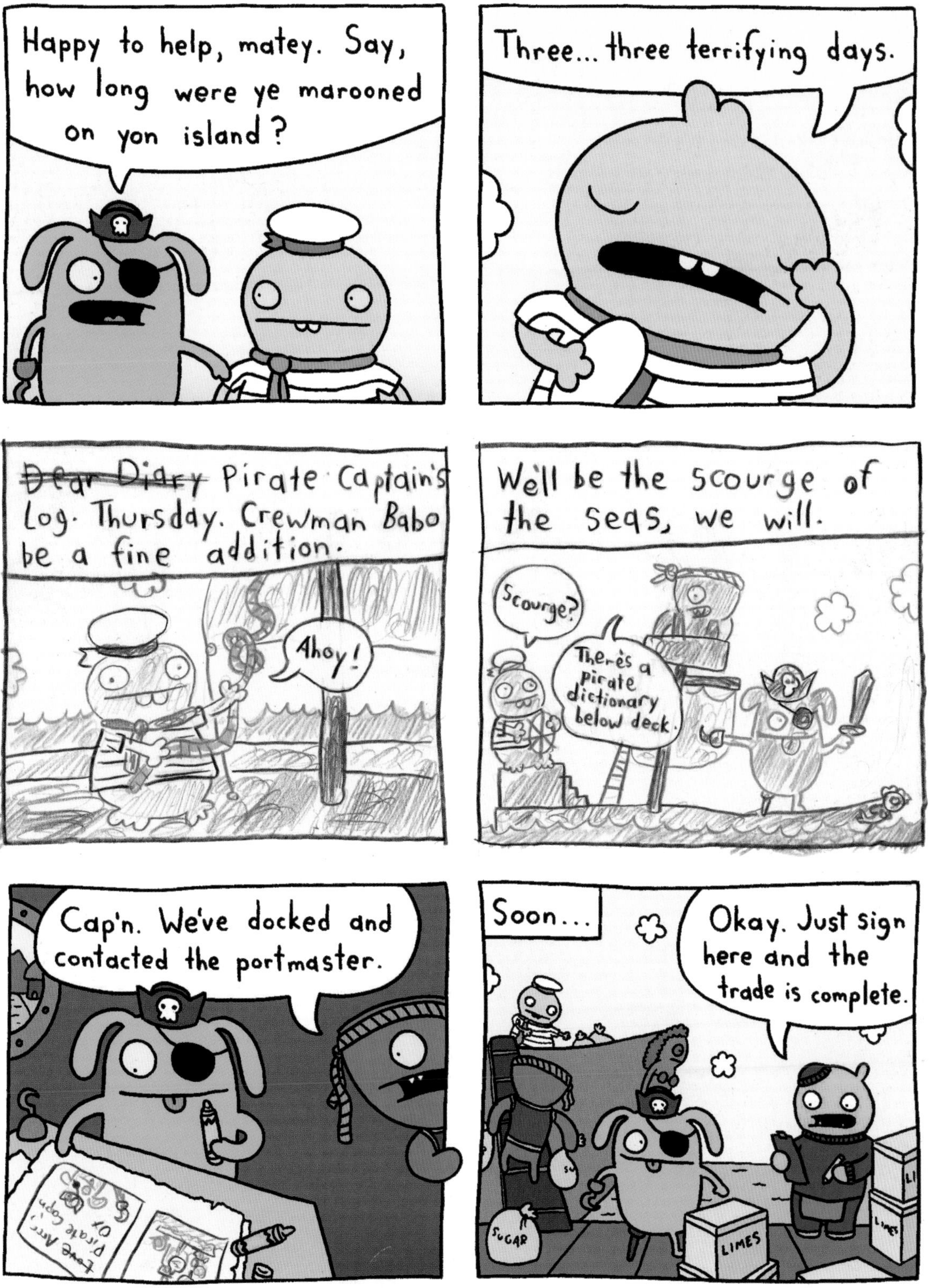
Happy to help, matey. Say, how long were ye marooned on yon island?
Three... three terrifying days.
~~Dear Diary~~ Pirate Captain's Log. Thursday. Crewman Babo be a fine addition.
Ahoy!
We'll be the scourge of the seas, we will.
Scourge?
There's a pirate dictionary below deck.
Cap'n. We've docked and contacted the portmaster.
Soon...
Okay. Just sign here and the trade is complete.
SUGAR
LIMES
LIMES

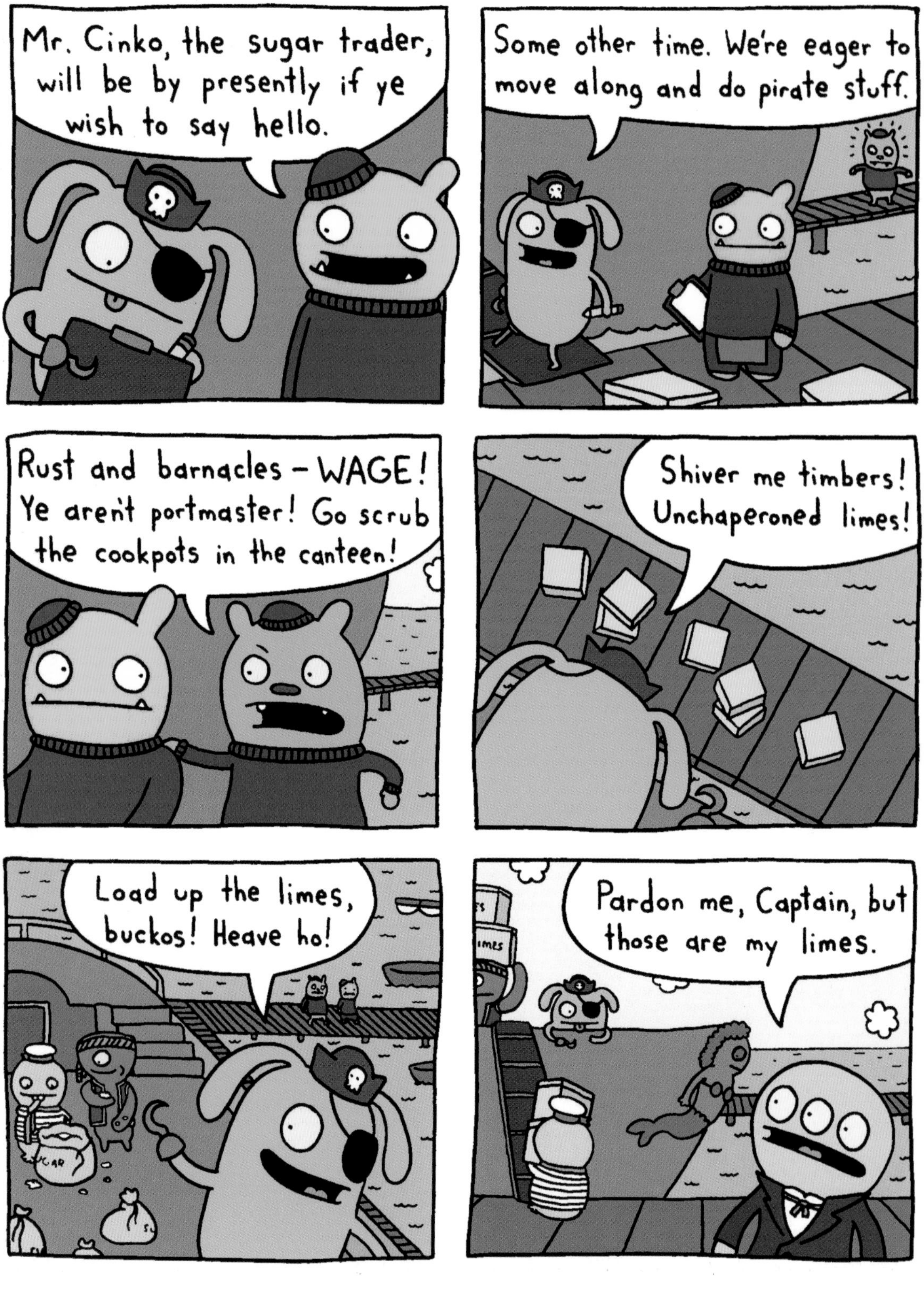
Mr. Cinko, the sugar trader, will be by presently if ye wish to say hello.
Some other time. We're eager to move along and do pirate stuff.
Rust and barnacles – WAGE! Ye aren't portmaster! Go scrub the cookpots in the canteen!
Shiver me timbers! Unchaperoned limes!
Load up the limes, buckos! Heave ho!
Pardon me, Captain, but those are my limes.

Ye must be mistaken. They're on my ship. But ye should join the crew!

I can't. I'm afraid of... that is, I don't have my sea legs. But my limes...

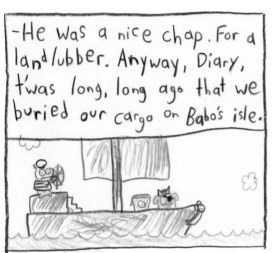

—He was a nice chap. For a landlubber. Anyway, Diary, t'was long, long ago that we buried our cargo on Babo's isle.

And now we have returned to collect our booty for another trade.

I don't get it. We buried the limes right here. Where did all of these trees come from, eh?

BONK!

finito, matey!

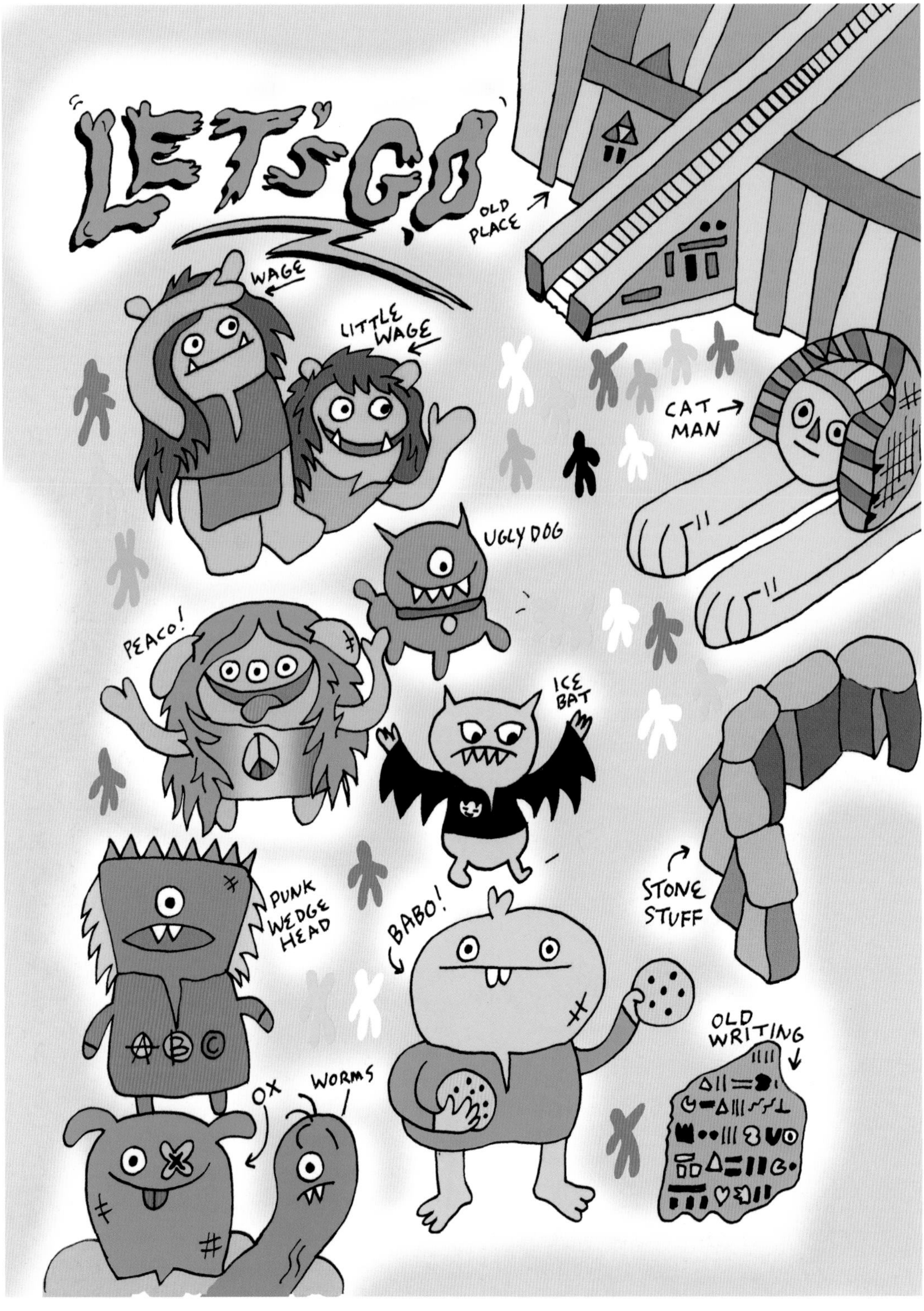
LET'S GO
OLD PLACE
WAGE
LITTLE WAGE
CAT MAN
UGLY DOG
PEACO!
ICE BAT
STONE STUFF
PUNK WEDGE HEAD
BABO!
OLD WRITING
OX
WORMS

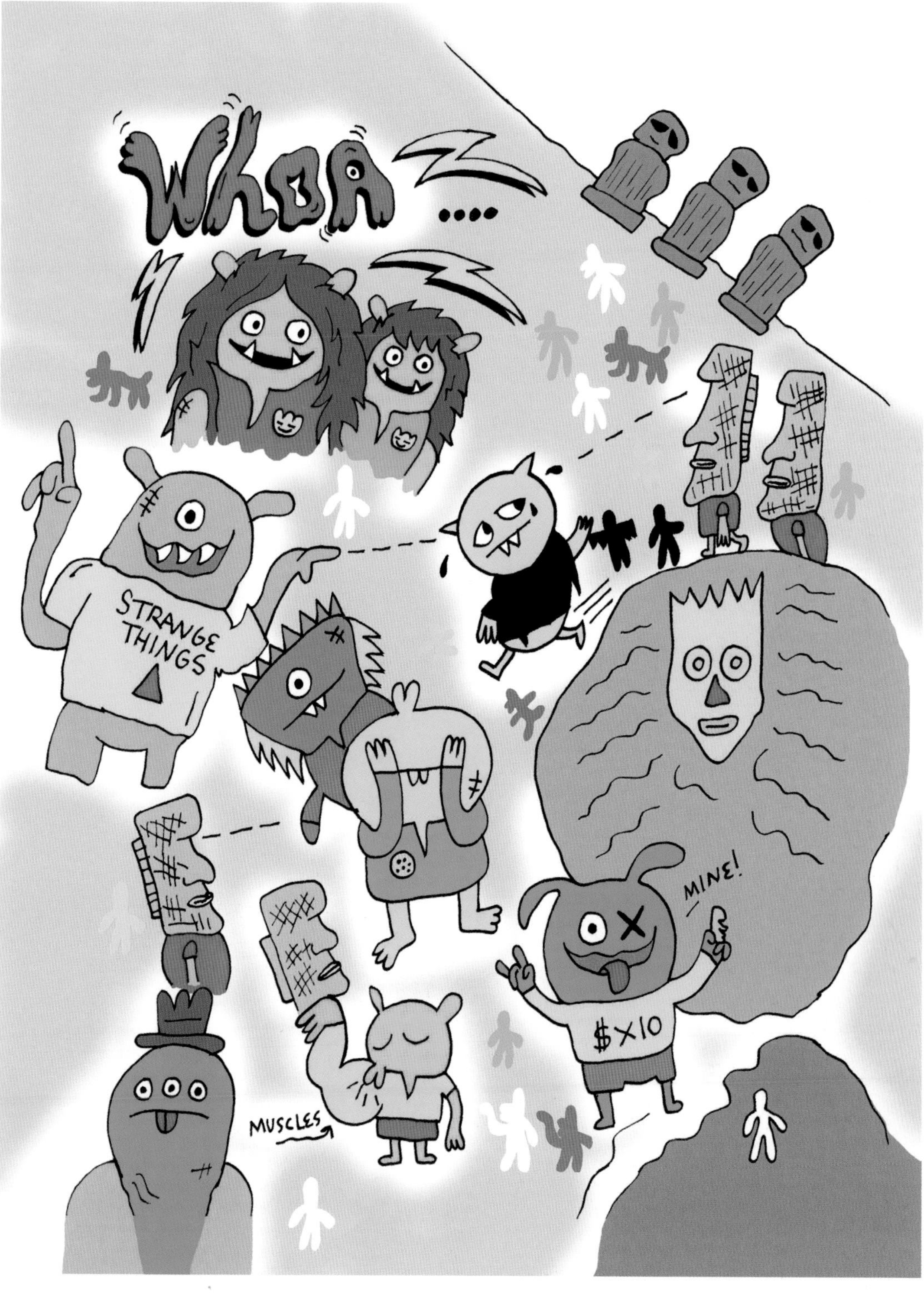
WHOA....
STRANGE THINGS
MINE!
$×10
MUSCLES

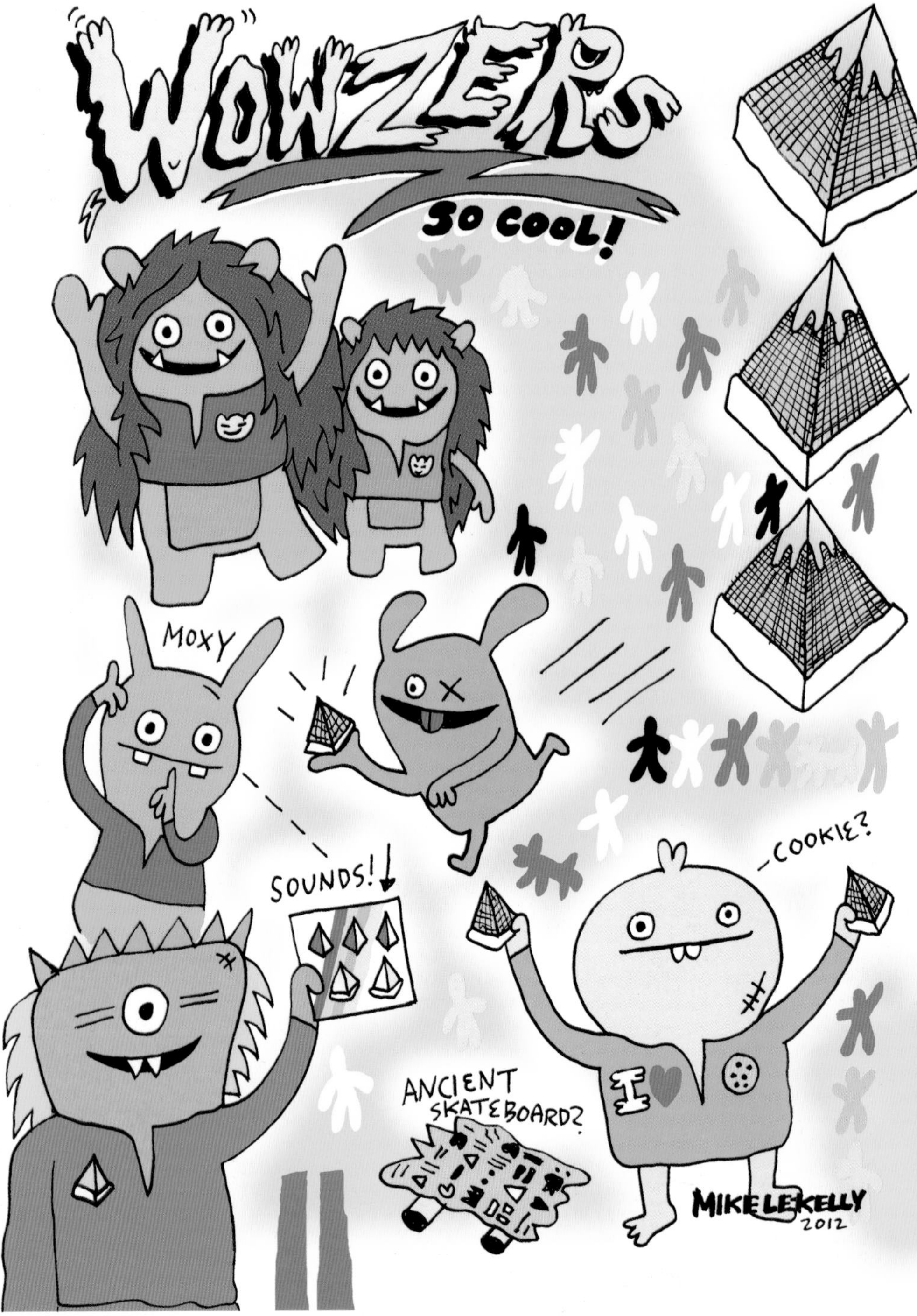
WOWZERS
SO COOL!
MOXY
SOUNDS!
-COOKIE?
ANCIENT SKATEBOARD?
MIKE LEKELLY 2012

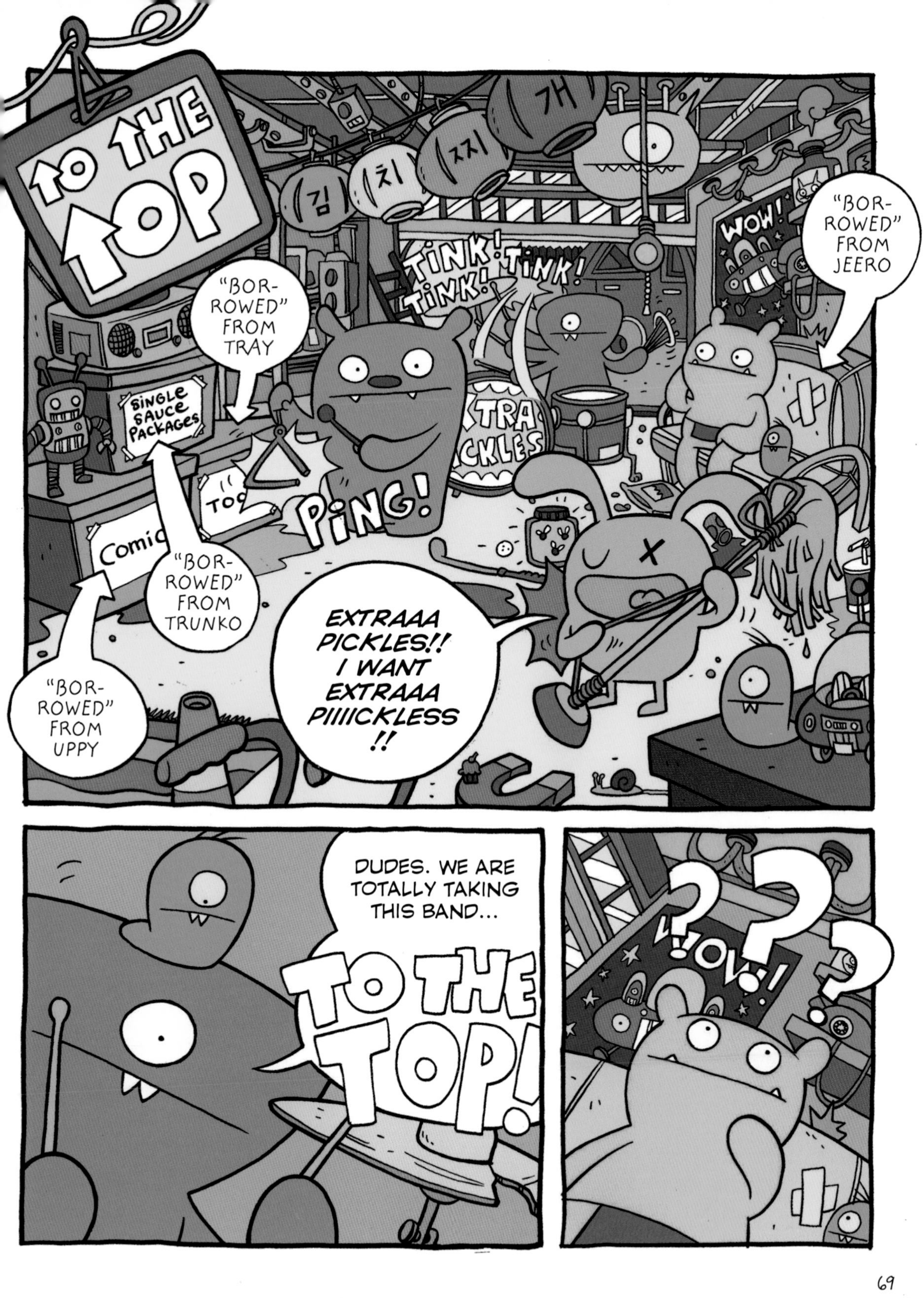
TO THE TOP
김 치 찌 개
TINK! TINK! TINK!
WOW!
"BOR-ROWED" FROM TRAY
"BOR-ROWED" FROM JEERO
SINGLE SAUCE PACKAGES
Comic
PING!
"BOR-ROWED" FROM TRUNKO
"BOR-ROWED" FROM UPPY
EXTRAAA PICKLES!! I WANT EXTRAAA PIIIICKLESS !!
DUDES. WE ARE TOTALLY TAKING THIS BAND...
TO THE TOP!
? ? ?

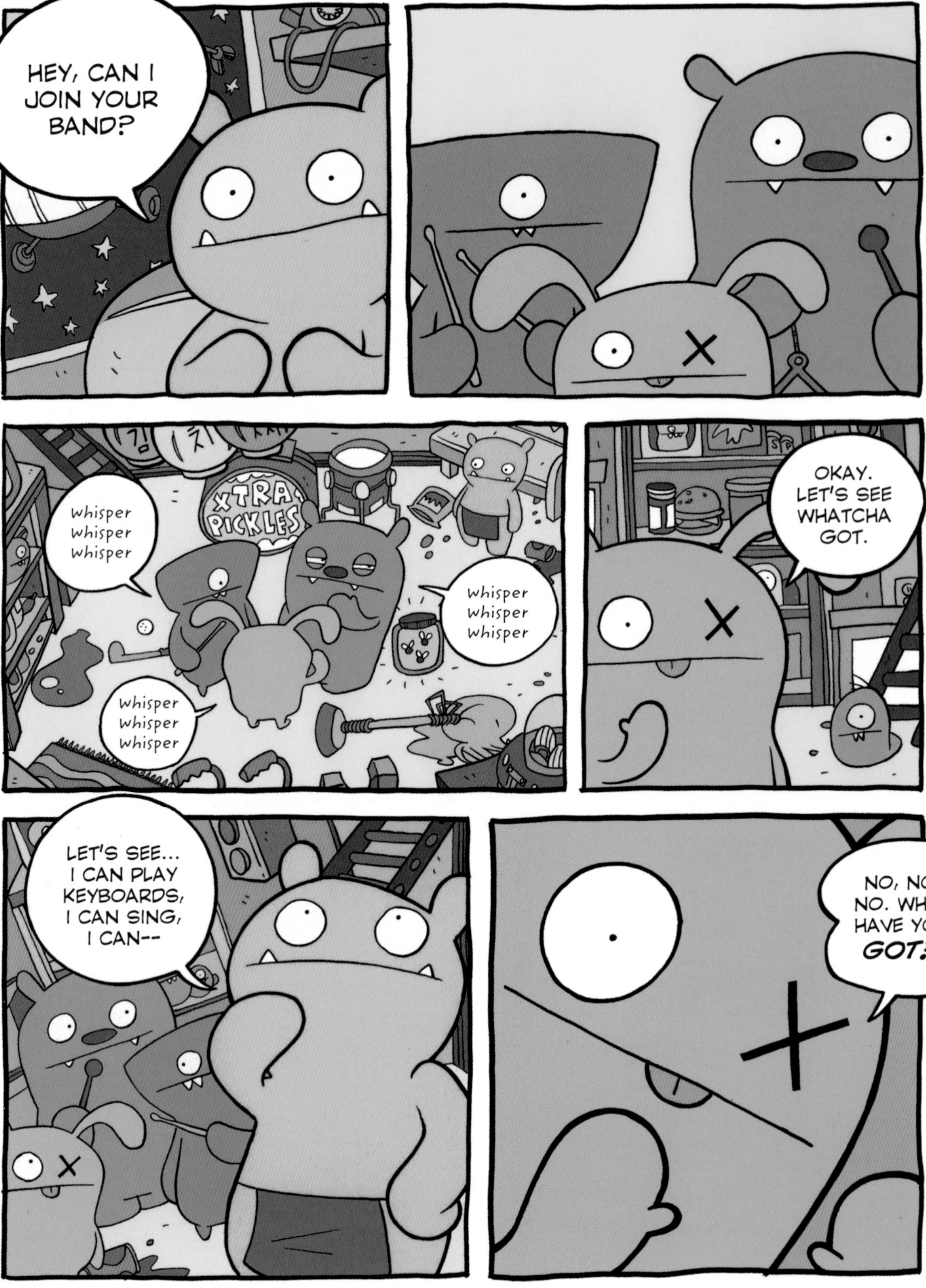
HEY, CAN I JOIN YOUR BAND?
whisper whisper whisper
whisper whisper whisper
whisper whisper whisper
XTRA PICKLES
OKAY. LET'S SEE WHATCHA GOT.
LET'S SEE... I CAN PLAY KEYBOARDS, I CAN SING, I CAN--
NO, NO, NO. WHA HAVE YOU GOT?

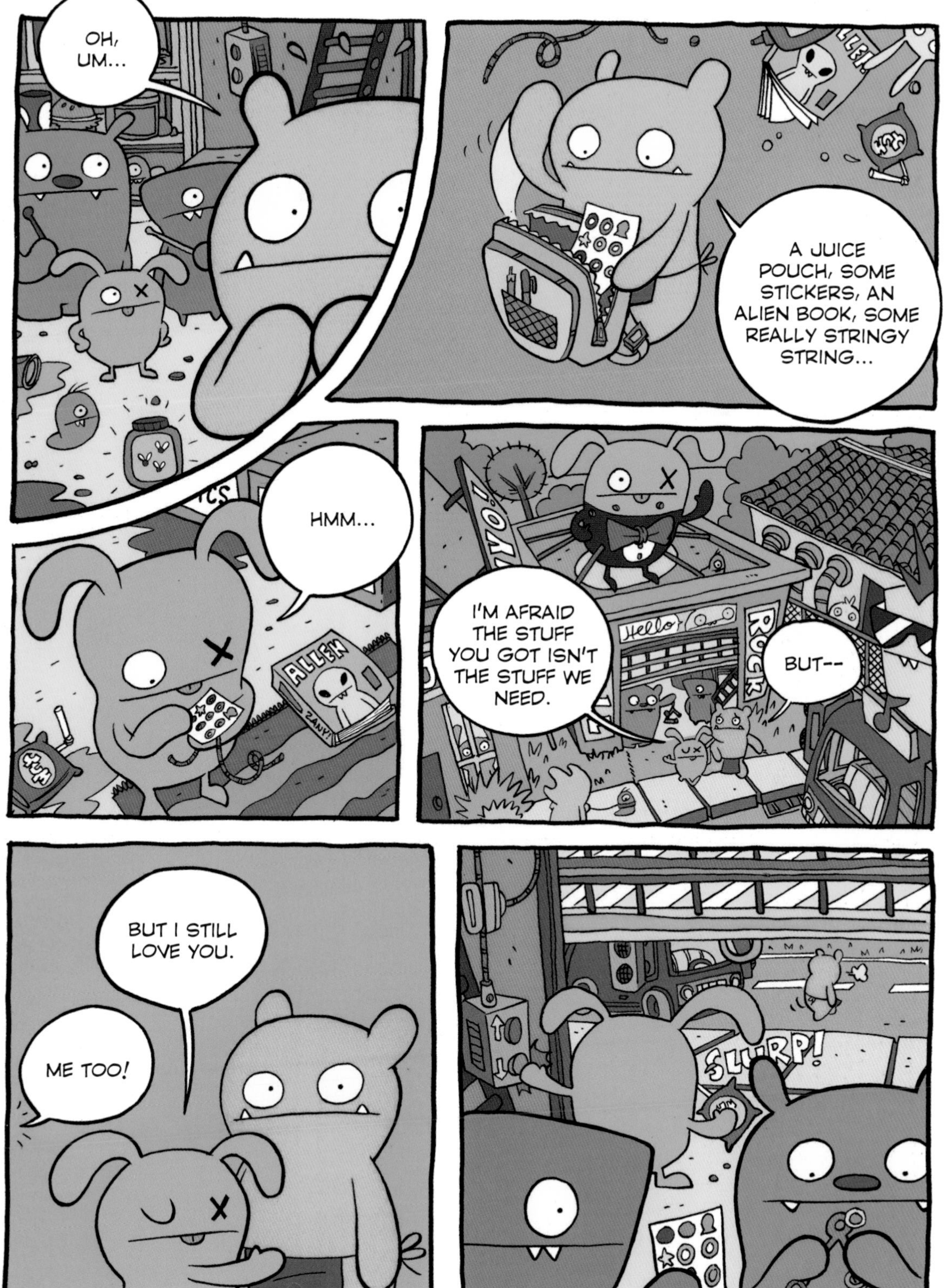
OH, UM...
A JUICE POUCH, SOME STICKERS, AN ALIEN BOOK, SOME REALLY STRINGY STRING...
ALIEN
HMM...
ALIEN
ZANY!
I'M AFRAID THE STUFF YOU GOT ISN'T THE STUFF WE NEED.
BUT--
Hello
ROCK
BUT I STILL LOVE YOU.
ME TOO!
SLURP!

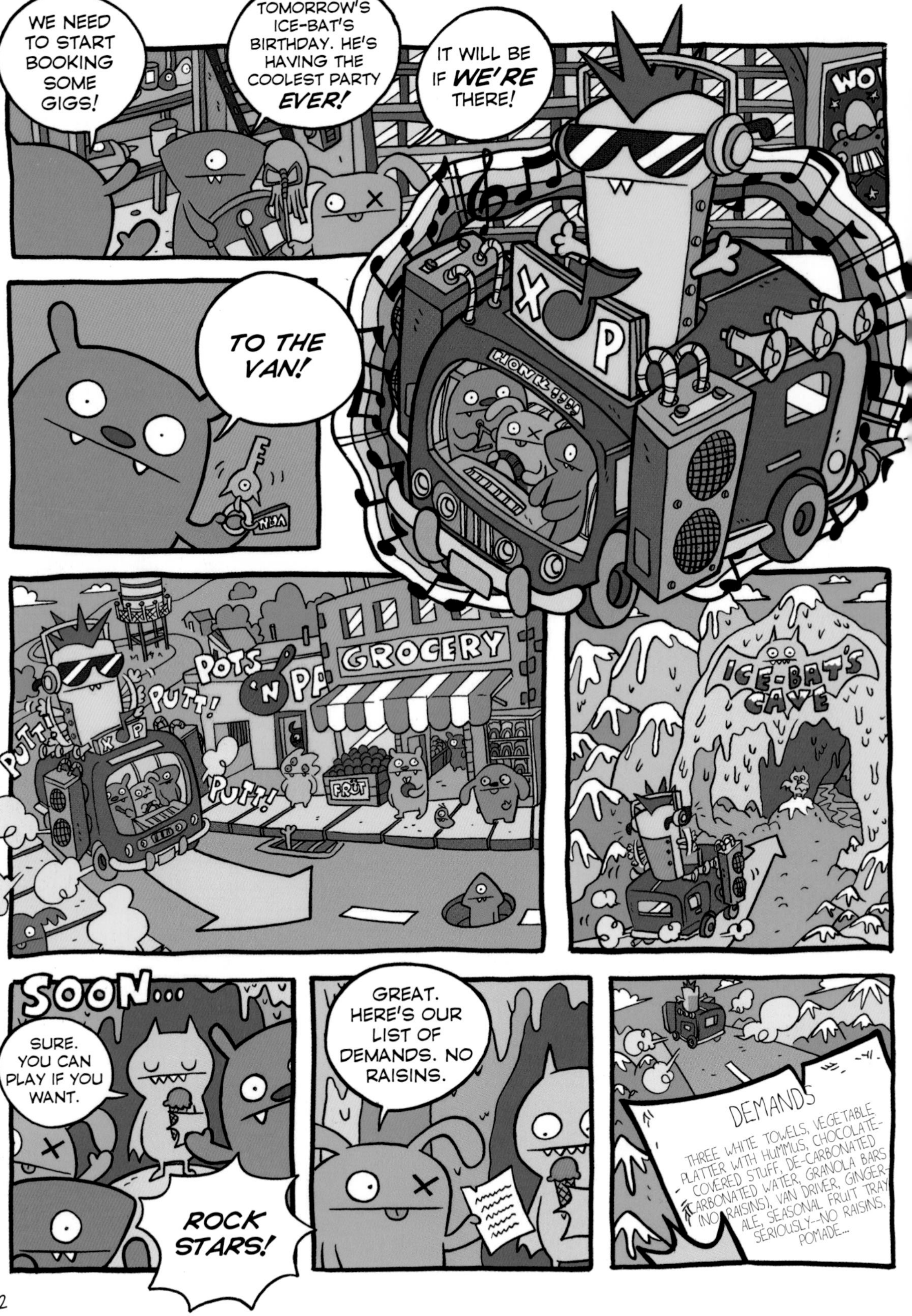
WE NEED TO START BOOKING SOME GIGS!
TOMORROW'S ICE-BAT'S BIRTHDAY. HE'S HAVING THE COOLEST PARTY EVER!
IT WILL BE IF WE'RE THERE!
TO THE VAN!
GROCERY
POTS 'N PA
PUTT!
PUTT!
PUTT!
FRUT
ICE-BAT'S CAVE
SOON...
SURE. YOU CAN PLAY IF YOU WANT.
ROCK STARS!
GREAT. HERE'S OUR LIST OF DEMANDS. NO RAISINS.
DEMANDS
THREE WHITE TOWELS, VEGETABLE PLATTER WITH HUMMUS, CHOCOLATE-COVERED STUFF, DE-CARBONATED CARBONATED WATER, GRANOLA BARS (NO RAISINS), VAN DRIVER, GINGER-ALE, SEASONAL FRUIT TRAY, SERIOUSLY--NO RAISINS, POMADE...

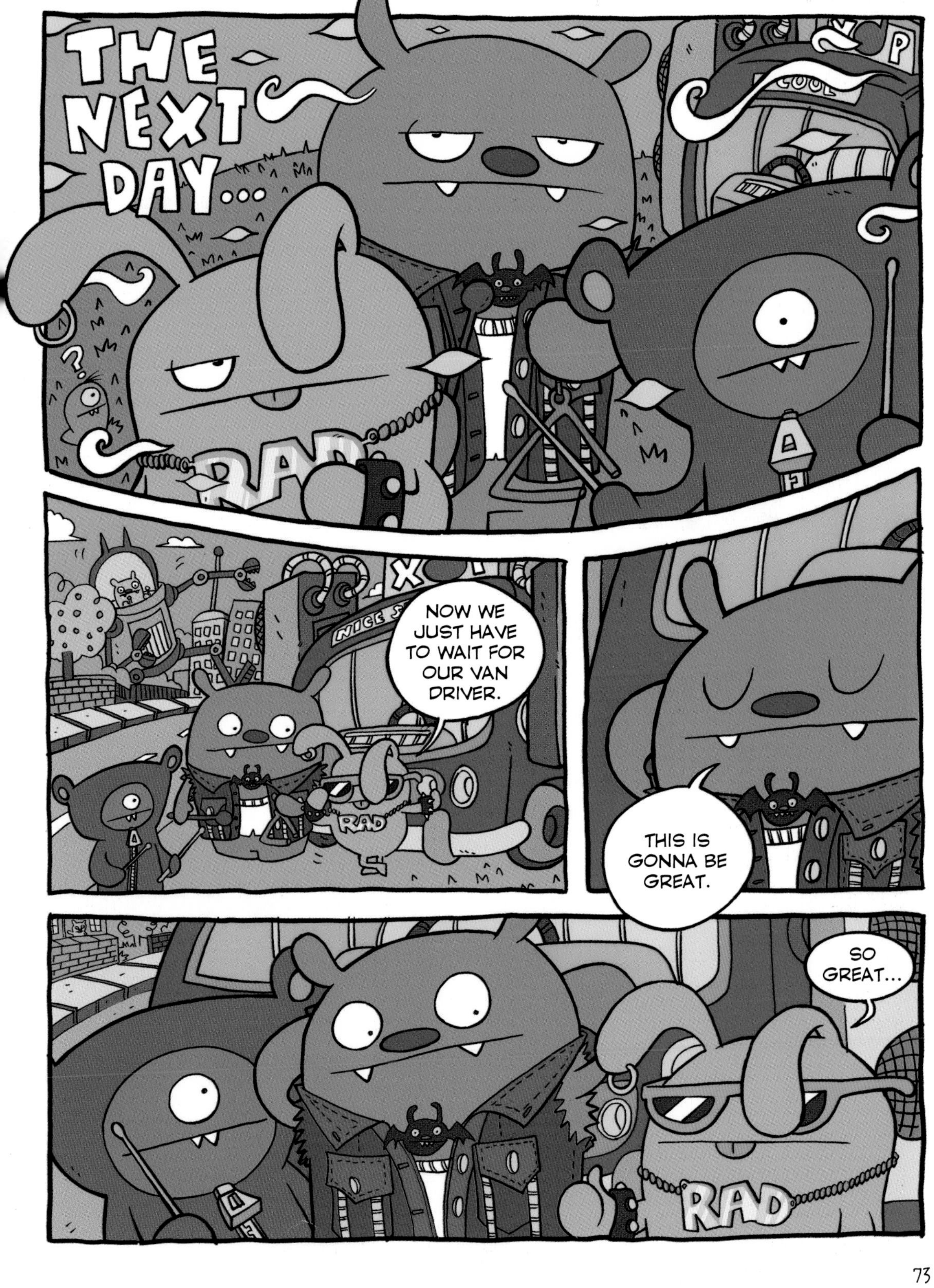
THE NEXT DAY...
RAD
NOW WE JUST HAVE TO WAIT FOR OUR VAN DRIVER.
THIS IS GONNA BE GREAT.
SO GREAT...
RAD

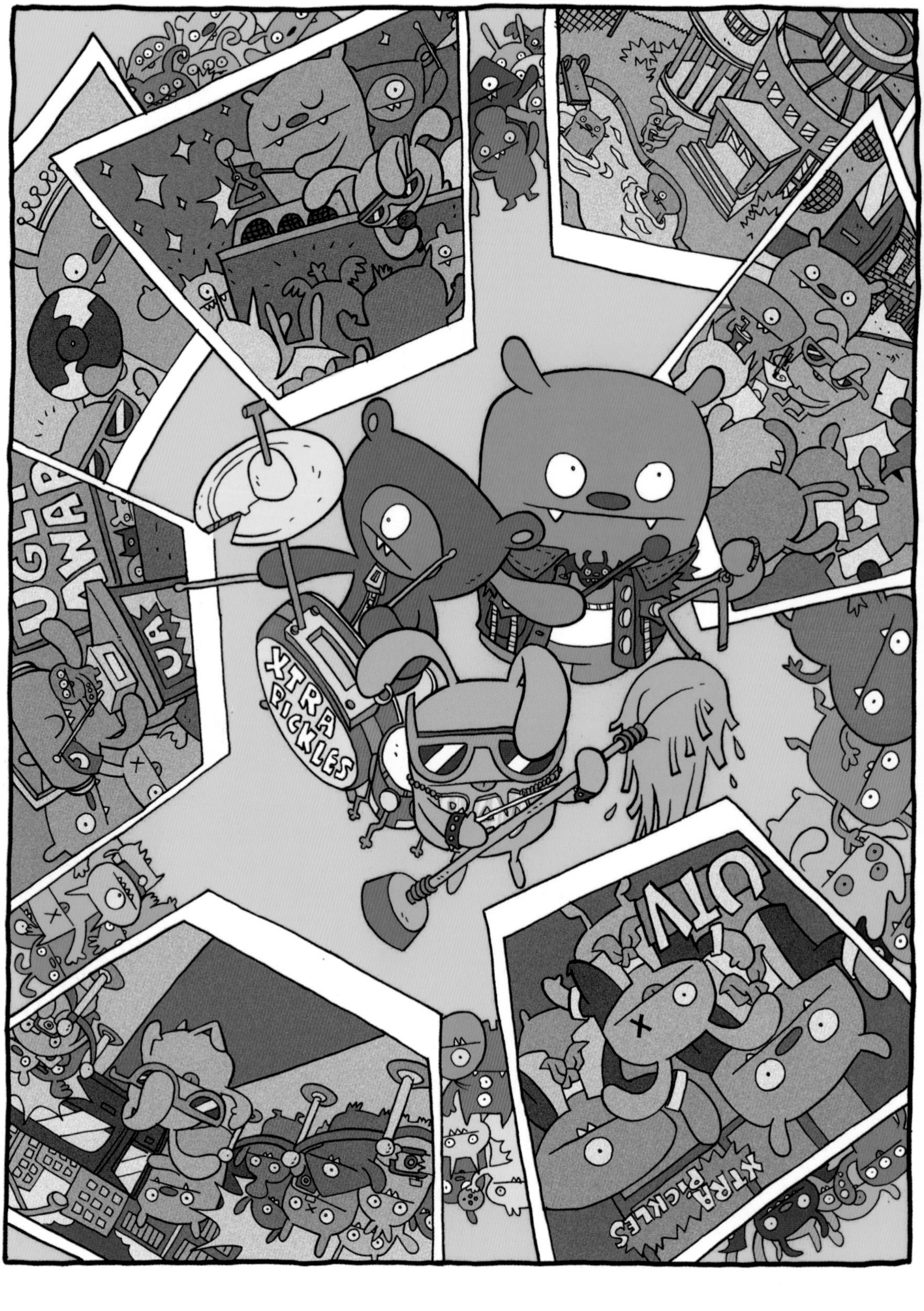
XTRA PICKLES
UGLY AWAR
UA
UTV
XTRA PICKLES

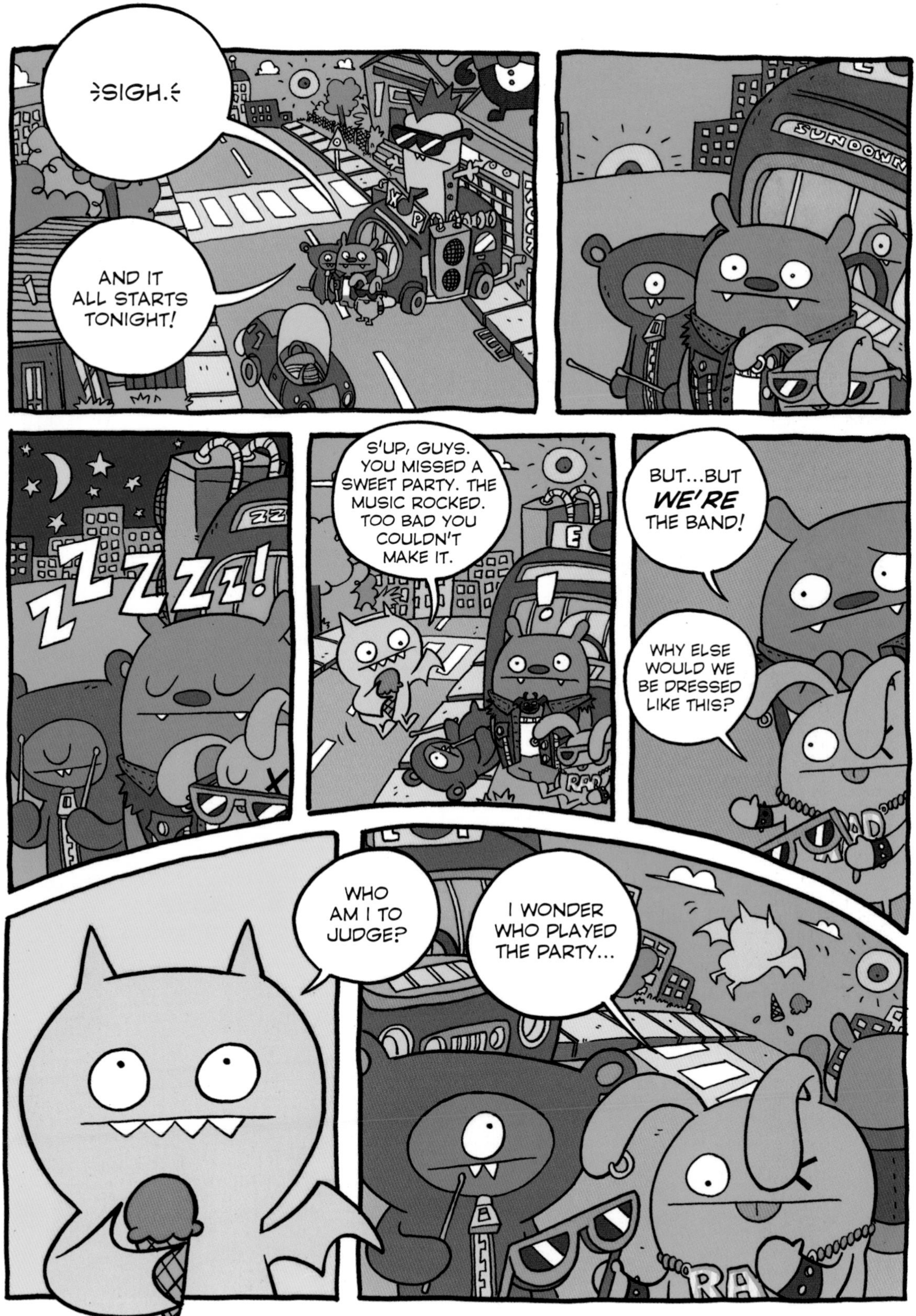

SIGH.
AND IT ALL STARTS TONIGHT!
SUNDOWN
ZZZZZ!
S'UP, GUYS. YOU MISSED A SWEET PARTY. THE MUSIC ROCKED. TOO BAD YOU COULDN'T MAKE IT.
!
BUT...BUT ***WE'RE*** THE BAND!
WHY ELSE WOULD WE BE DRESSED LIKE THIS?
WHO AM I TO JUDGE?
I WONDER WHO PLAYED THE PARTY...

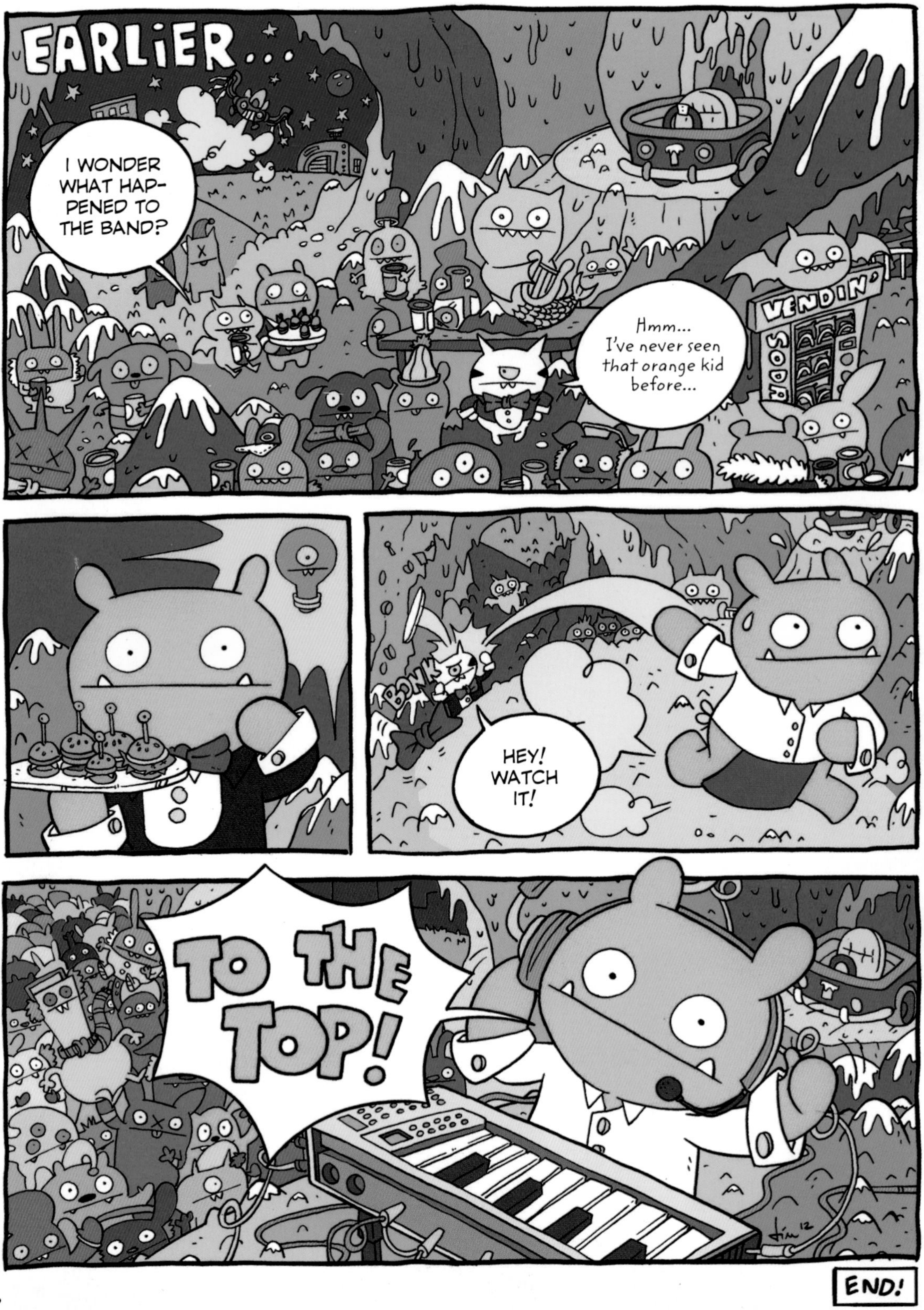
EARLIER...
I WONDER WHAT HAPPENED TO THE BAND?
Hmm... I've never seen that orange kid before...
VENDIN'
SODA
BONK
HEY! WATCH IT!
TO THE TOP!
END!

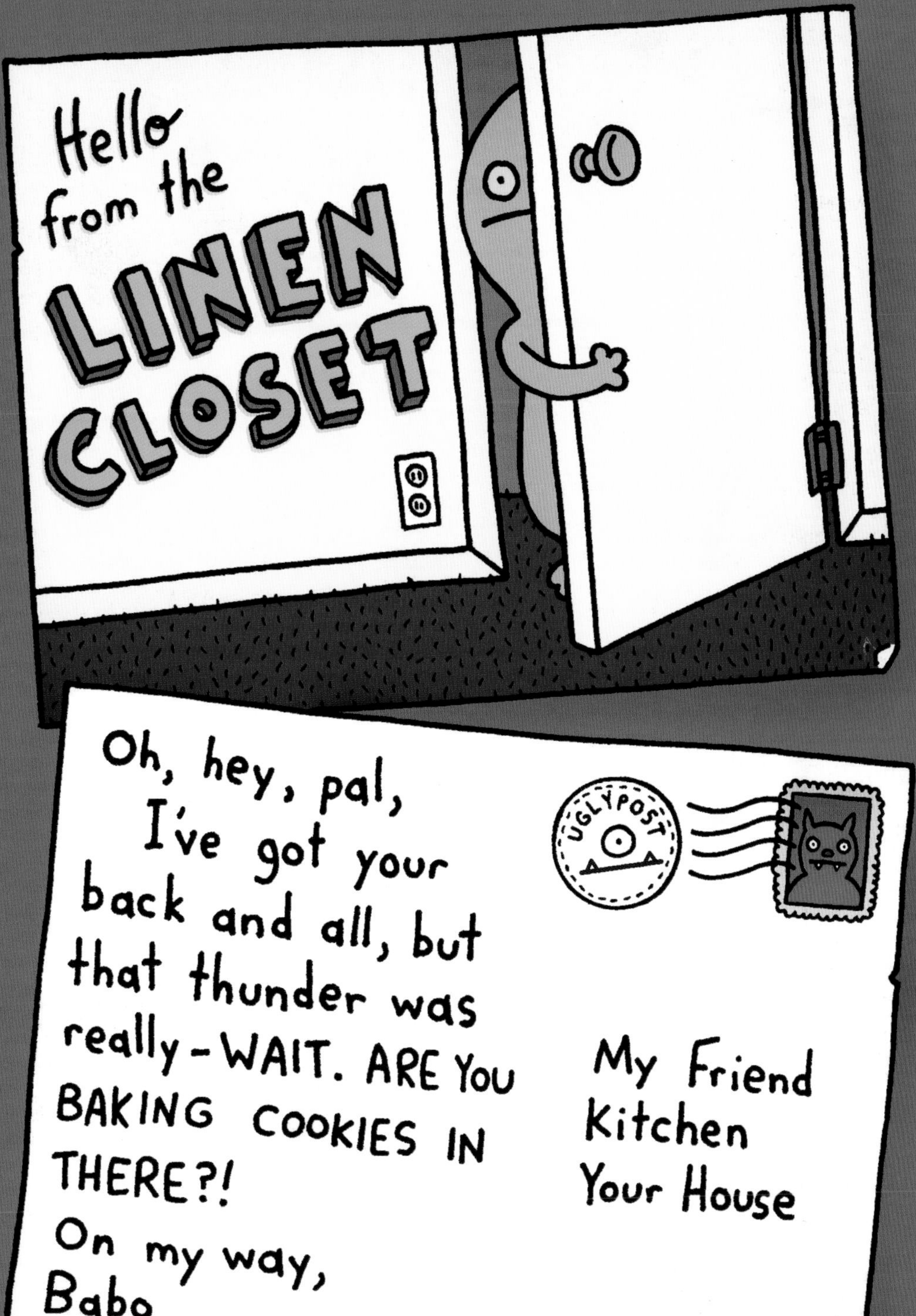
Hello from the
LINEN CLOSET
Oh, hey, pal,
I've got your back and all, but that thunder was really-WAIT. ARE YOU BAKING COOKIES IN THERE?!
On my way,
Babo
UGLYPOST
My Friend
Kitchen
Your House

BROUGHT

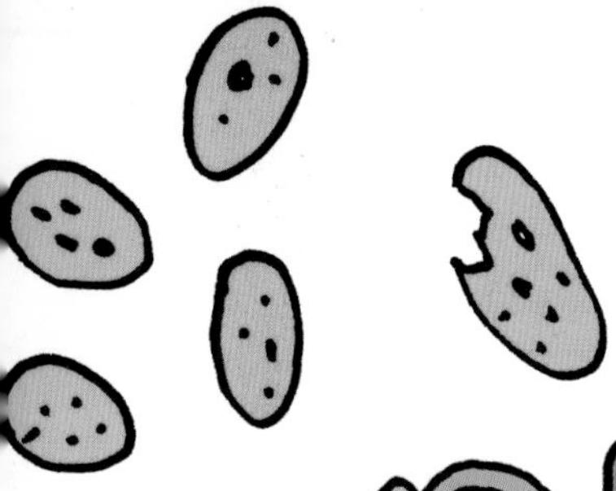

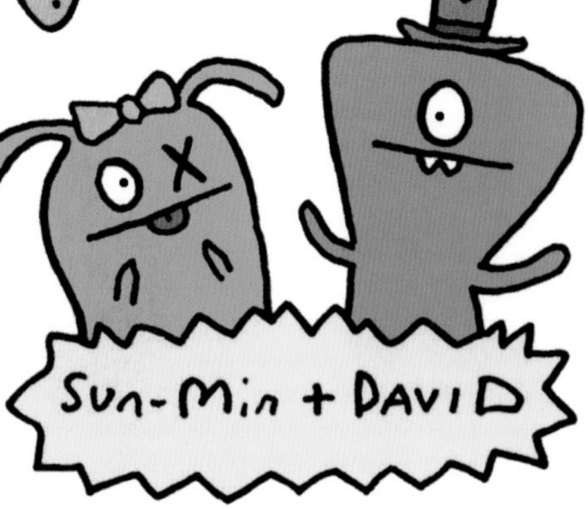
Sun-Min + DAVID

SUN-MIN KIM & DAVID HORVATH

are best known for creating the world of Uglydoll, which started as a line of handmade plush dolls and has since grown into a brand loved by all ages around the world. Their works can be found everywhere from the Moma in Tokyo and the Louvre in Paris, to the windows of their very own Uglydoll shop in Seoul. Sun-Min and David's very first conversation was about the meaning of "ugly." To them, ugly means unique and different, that which makes us who we are. It should never be hidden, but shouted from the rooftops! They wanted to build a world that showed the twists and turns that make us who we are, inside and out, because the whole world benefits when we embrace our true, twisty-turny selves. So, ugly is the new beauty. This Uglydoll comic features some of Sun-Min and David's heroes from the pop art and comic art world.

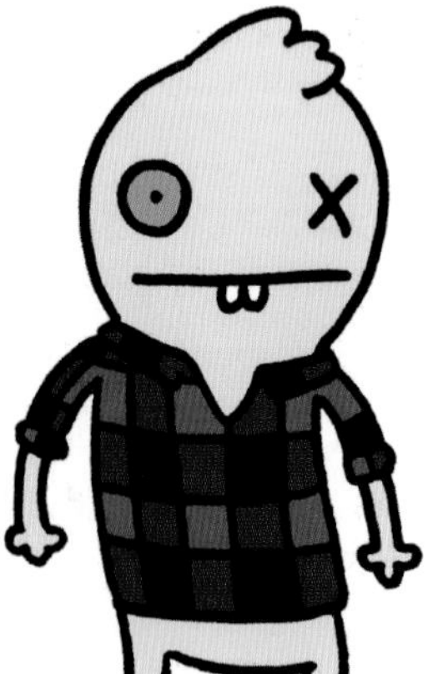

TRAVIS NICHOLS

is the author and illustrator of several books for kids and post-kids, including *The Monster Doodle Book*, *Punk Rock Etiquette* and *Matthew Meets the Man*. He previously drew comics for the late, great *Nickelodeon Magazine*. His deepest, most secret wish is to wake up as a gnome and spend his days building wooden locks, eating tiny biscuits and hanging out with birds. He can be found eating watermelon over the sink or online.

IAN MCGINTY

Comic Book Artist.
STR 8
WIS 10
INT 12
DEX 16
CON 13
CHA 14

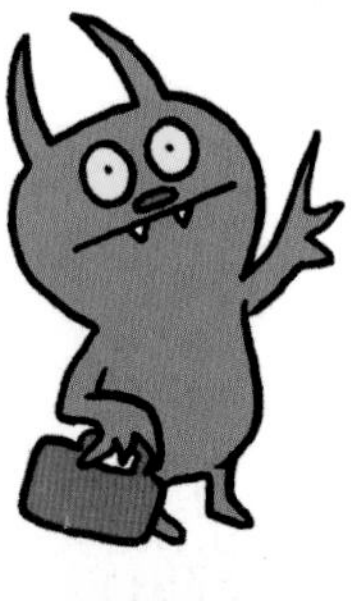

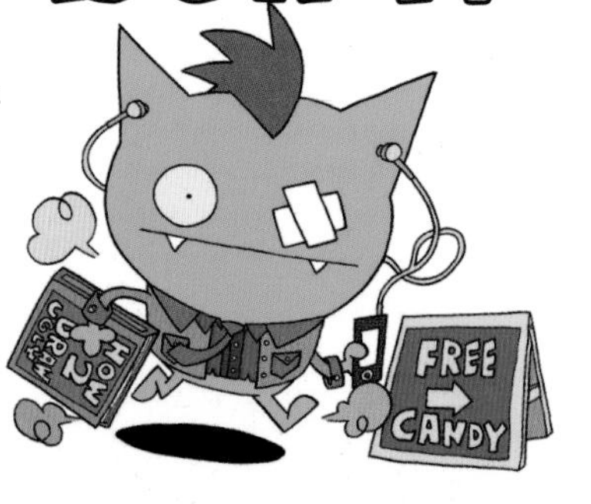
HOW 2
FREE
CANDY

TO YOU BY:

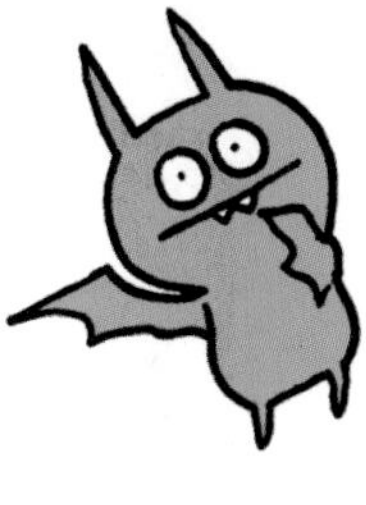

PHILLIP JACOBSON

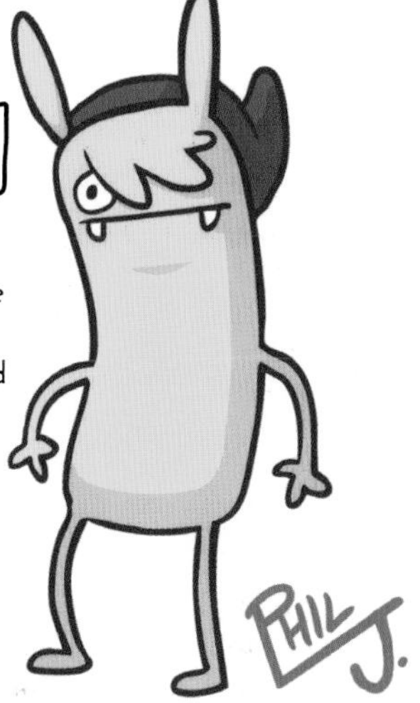
PHIL J.

is a 23-year-old graduate student at the Savannah College of Art and Design studying sequential art. His earlier works include the self-published titles Battle Mammals and Pancakes for Yeti. Some of his influences include Bryan Lee O'Malley, Madeline Rupert, and Craig Bartlett. He would like to thank his late grandmother Mary Ann Hill for constantly encouraging him to draw when he was little and for inspiring him to pursue his artistic goals.

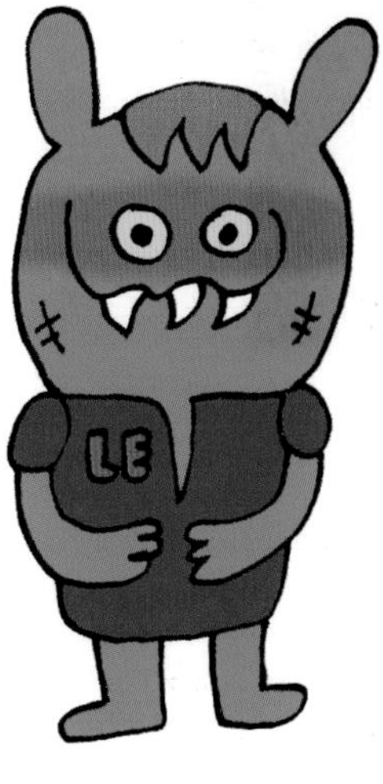
LE

MIKE LE KELLY

is a Seattle-based artist. His work ranges from illustrations, toys and sculpture to hand-cast resin figures. He draws inspiration from scary movies from his VHS collection to 70s rock and boogie. He believes in the notion that YOU MUST CREATE.

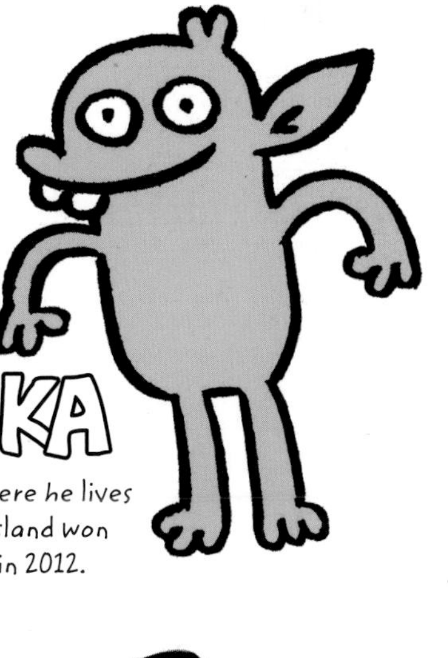

JAMES KOCHALKA

is the Cartoonist Laureate of the state of Vermont, where he lives with his wife and two boys. His book Dragon Puncher Island won an Eisner Award for best publication for early readers in 2012.

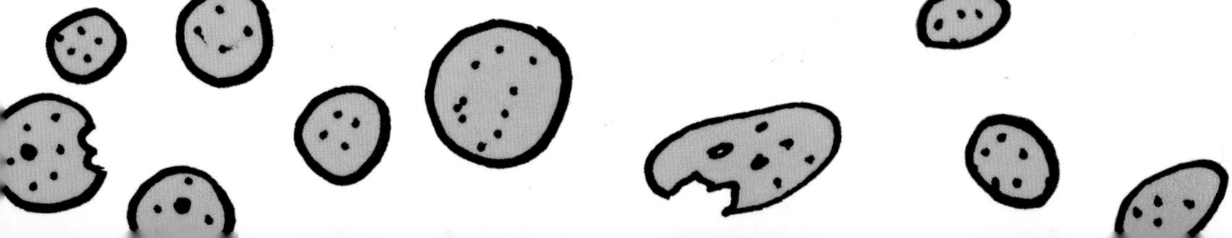

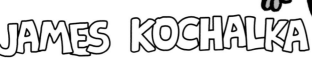

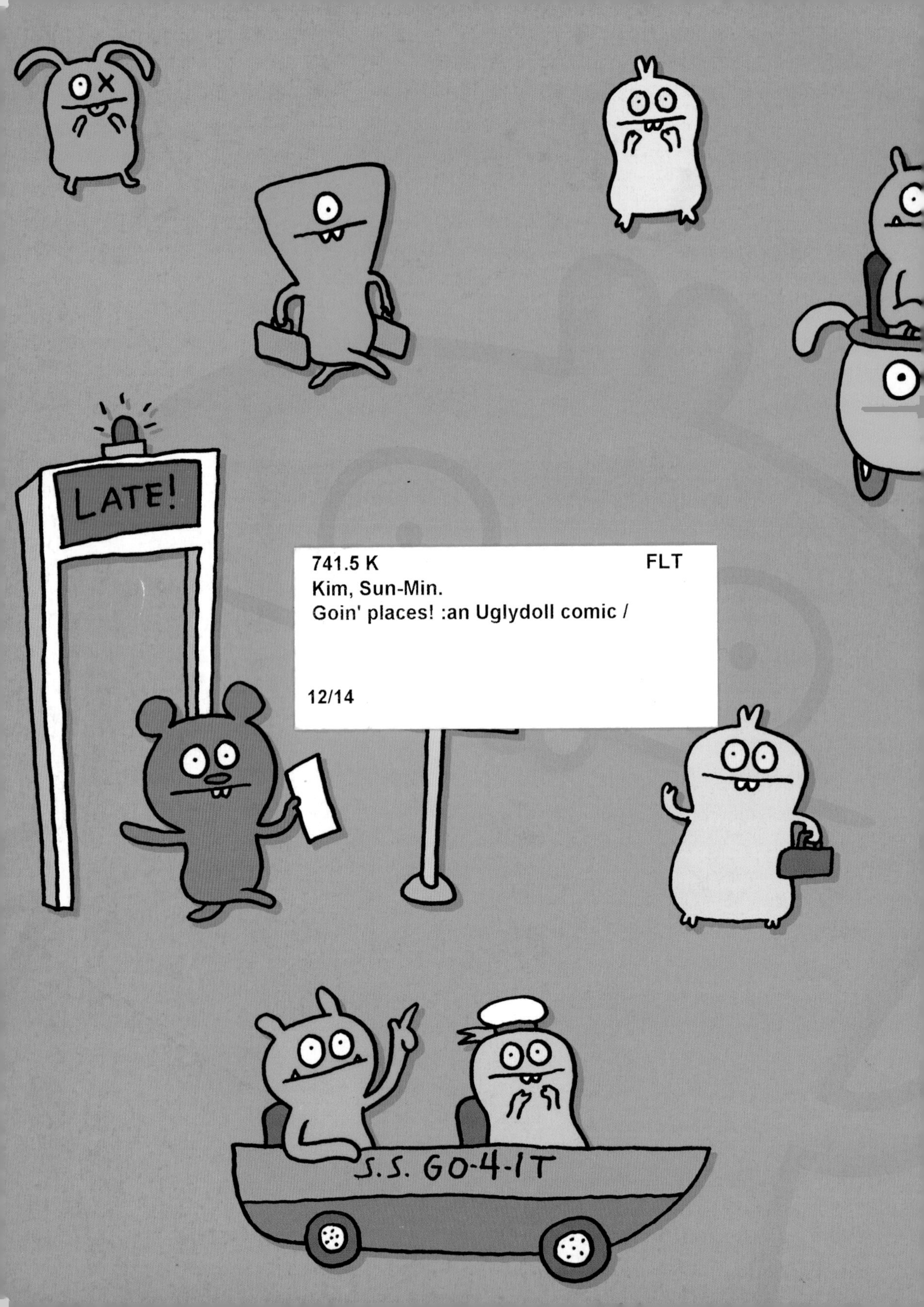
LATE!
S.S. GO-4-IT